RAINBOWS & LOVE SONGS

Kacy Angelle would never forget the stranger's eyes. They held more emotion than she could fathom. She watched as he argued with the loan officer at one of Houston's savings and loans. Weeks later, she ran into the stranger again. Dan Wilder couldn't believe his rotten luck. He was on the verge of righting a treacherous wrong when this doe-eyed woman came along and caught him in the act. Worst of all, she could identify him. He had to take her hostage . . .

Books by Catherine Sellers
in the Linford Romance Library:

ALWAYS

CATHERINE SELLERS

RAINBOWS
&
LOVE SONGS

Complete and Unabridged

LINFORD
Leicester

First published in the
United States of America

First Linford Edition
published 2002

British Library CIP Data

Sellers, Catherine
 Rainbows & love songs.—Large print ed.—
 Linford romance library
 1. Love stories
 2. Large type books
 I. Title
 813.5′4 [F]

 ISBN 0–7089–9895–X

Published by
F. A. Thorpe (Publishing)
Anstey, Leicestershire

Set by Words & Graphics Ltd.
Anstey, Leicestershire
Printed and bound in Great Britain by
T. J. International Ltd., Padstow, Cornwall

This book is printed on acid-free paper

For Lis, who knows the true
meaning of friendship.
And for Bill.

1

Kacy Angelle glanced down at the Timex on her wrist, probably for the twentieth time, and felt her eyebrows pull together in irritation. Arriving ten minutes early for her one-thirty appointment, she'd been waiting well over forty-five minutes, time enough to come to the conclusion that bankers were as insensitive to the importance of others' time as were doctors.

What's more, Southside Savings and Loan of Houston, Texas, was the last place she needed to be at twelve past two in the afternoon. Mary, her friend and partner, and their helpers, Tina and Justine, would soon have their hands full getting twenty-two preschoolers up from their afternoon nap. Kacy hated leaving her co-workers shorthanded, but someone had to take care of this unexpected foul-up.

A shiver laced with foreboding sliced through her. She tried to rationalize it by telling herself that it was only her reaction to all the glass and chrome and black vinyl that surrounded her. But the premonition of impending disaster was too strong to ignore altogether.

Unconsciously she clutched the envelope in her hands so tightly that she had to lay it in her lap and smooth it back into shape. The future of Wee Care Day Care depended on Kacy keeping both a clear head and her cool. More important, Mandy's adoption depended on Wee Care's continued success.

Mandy. Just the name conjured up images of big brown eyes, a snaggle-toothed grin that tugged at the heart, and tiny fingers that felt so small yet so comforting in her own. Kacy smiled to herself, remembering how lonely her life had been before her cousin's daughter had filled her world with laughter and warmth and a sense of deep and abiding worth. After so many years of being on her own, it was good to be important in someone else's life. Mandy needed her, and, for the moment, that was enough.

'Sir, wait!'

Kacy glanced up to see the receptionist skirting her desk in a frantic attempt to stop the man who had obviously bypassed her station. Kacy wasn't sure what she expected next, but to her way of thinking the petite blonde was making a grave mistake by placing her body between the six-footer and the door stenciled *Marcus Hawkins — Loan Officer*. Even at five-nine, Kacy never would have entertained the notion of tangling with a man of his stature, especially one who looked like he was bent on destruction.

'You can't go in there,' the young woman in the trim black skirt and white silk blouse insisted.

'The hell I can't.' He started past her again. Still, she barred his path.

'These people,' she said, with a gesture toward Kacy and the three men sitting in the second-story reception

3

area, 'have appointments and have been waiting for quite some time.'

Kacy had banked at Southside ever since her divorce eleven years ago. She knew that the receptionist was new, which had to account for her fool-hardy approach to the situation. A more experienced woman would have called Security.

The thought popped right out of her brain, however, the instant the man turned his head toward the group of startled onlookers. His gaze zeroed in on Kacy — and her breath got lost somewhere in her chest.

'This won't take long,' he said to no one but her. Not even the edge of hostility in his words could disguise the velvet-soft timbre of his voice. But it was his eyes, the color of a tempestuous sea, that held sway over the moment. Never had she been so affected by the mere physical presence of one person, and, she realized with growing discomfort, she could not make herself look away.

Apparently he labored under no such handicap. Turning his attention back to the girl before him, he spoke, and although Kacy couldn't hear his words, she saw the immediate change in the girl's demeanor. Kacy wasn't surprised that she didn't object to being escorted back to her desk, where he placed both his hands on her shoulders and gently but firmly forced her down into her chair. Kacy felt a sudden surge of empathy for the young girl; she knew firsthand what it was like to be intimidated into submission by size and physical strength.

'Stay put,' he ordered with a glower that would have nailed any man his own size to the wall. The receptionist did as he instructed, then they all watched him stride past to shove open the door to Marcus Hawkins' office.

'What the hell do you want, Wild — '
The door slammed shut, effectively cutting off Marcus Hawkins' nasal twang, a twang made more pronounced by the note of surprise in his voice.

Then, scuffling sounds and angry voices too muffled to be intelligible filtered through the closed door. The exchange heated at a rapid rate, then loud thuds erupted, thuds that sounded like a body being slammed against a wall.

Unwanted and unbidden, flashes from the past invaded Kacy's mind — every unwarranted accusation, every degrading name Ted had called her assaulted her now as he had on those two occasions during their one-year marriage — until she shoved them back to where she kept them carefully and deeply buried. She wasn't eighteen anymore, and the divorce was long behind her.

Alarmed, she glanced first at the men around her, then at the frightened girl behind the desk. No one made a move to help. It was obvious, at least to Kacy, that if she didn't do something, Marcus Hawkins was in deep trouble. Hurriedly she made her way to the reception desk.

'Call Security,' Kacy said in a loud

whisper. At last, the receptionist came out of her stupor. She took the phone Kacy handed her and punched a series of numbers, swore, then hung up and tried again.

'Don't think this is over, Hawkins.'

Both women looked up when the door swung open, and the dark-haired stranger stalked back out into the waiting area. His jacket hung off one broad shoulder, but he didn't seem to notice, much less care. Instead, he turned his unyielding glare on the girl at the desk. Her finger stopped in mid-punch.

'That won't be necessary,' he said with such authority that she placed the receiver back in its cradle. He stood so close now that Kacy smelled his cologne. It was an intoxicating fragrance, one she recognized but didn't have time to put a name to. She knew before it happened that his next comment would be to her.

'You got business with that son of a bitch?' Thick dark brows knitted together to furrow his sun-bronzed forehead.

Again Kacy found it impossible to tear her eyes from his. The muscles along his jawline tensed, drawing her attention to his chiseled features, features that were too rugged to be considered handsome, but features that made up a face she found surprisingly appealing.

In spite of needing a haircut and a shave, he didn't fit the stereotype of a ruffian. His black three-piece suit fit as if it had been tailor-made for him. The whiteness of his unbuttoned shirt stood out in stark relief against his dark skin, and his hair came as close to black as any she'd ever seen. Still, it was his eyes that captured her attention, for they held more emotion than Kacy could fathom. The two that she recognized immediately were rage and hatred. Eleven years after the nightmare and she was still an expert in seeing the warning signals. What had Marcus Hawkins done to warrant such

8

contempt? But beneath the fury she sensed more, something she couldn't quite define yet was so tangible that she felt drawn by it. There was no doubt in her mind that he was suffering. From what she had no way of knowing, but she found herself wanting to do something to assuage his distress. While she prided herself in being objective in her impressions of people, this stranger with his turbulent green eyes and enigmatic demeanor affected her like no other man ever had.

Amazed at how much detail she managed to absorb in so short a span of time — she'd even noticed his tie peeking out of his jacket pocket — she realized she hadn't answered his question. She gave him a quick nod.

'Do yourself a favor,' he said, his gaze riveting her again. 'Take your business elsewhere.' The words were hardly spoken before he brushed past her to step into the waiting elevator. The doors closed, leaving the reception area quieter than it had been moments

9

earlier — and its occupants to wonder if the incident had happened at all.

No one moved. No one spoke. Until Marcus Hawkins' voice squawked from behind them.

'Miss Ross!'

Five heads turned in unison to see the impeccably dressed but rumpled banker leaning against the doorjamb. His straight brown hair hung limply in his face. His tie looked as though it had been yanked to one side and then forgotten.

Only Miss Ross moved as she sprang to her feet. 'Are you all right?'

'Yes, yes, of course,' Hawkins grumbled with a well-aimed glower. 'I thought I told you I didn't want to see that man again.'

The unfairness of his reprimand incensed Kacy. What had he expected a girl half his own size to do when he had been so utterly defenseless himself?

'I . . . I'm sorry,' Miss Ross stammered, lowering her gaze when Hawkins turned his beady black eyes on her. 'I'll call Security if he — '

'No!' Hawkins cut her off, his dark eyes narrowing to reptilian slits. 'Just don't let him take me by surprise next time. And cancel the rest of my appointments.'

'But, Mr. Hawkins — ' Kacy's objection bounced off the slamming door.

None of the other patrons appeared unduly vexed by the inconvenience and filed toward the elevators. But Kacy's mission was of the utmost importance. With that thought uppermost, she turned back to Miss Ross, who was busy at her computer. She waited patiently for the girl to notice her.

When she didn't, Kacy cleared her throat and addressed her, 'Miss Ross.'

The receptionist jumped. 'Sorry,' she apologized. 'I guess I'm a little on edge.'

Kacy gave her a sympathetic smile. 'I understand. That was quite a commotion.'

'I'll say.' Miss Ross swiveled her chair

around to face Kacy fully. 'What can I do for you, Miss . . . ?'

'Angelle.' Kacy took the letter out of its envelope and handed it to her. 'I have to see Mr. Hawkins about this. If I understand it right, it says that we have only six weeks to pay our loan balance in full.' She pointed to the distressing notice. 'That can't be right, and I need to get it corrected as soon as possible.'

'I see,' Miss Ross said thoughtfully, but Kacy doubted the young woman had a clue to the seriousness of her problem.

'My hours are pretty flexible, so any time he has free tomorrow will be okay.'

Miss Ross's pert features sagged with a frown. 'I'm afraid not. Today is Mr. Hawkins' last day at the office before his vacation. He won't be back until after Thanksgiving.'

'Thanksgiving?' Kacy couldn't conceal her disappointment. 'But that's more than three weeks away.'

'Won't do, huh?' Miss Ross glanced toward Hawkins's office, then swiveled back to her computer. 'Mr. Hawkins really doesn't like anyone snooping around in his accounts, but I'll see what the computer tells me.' After several unsuccessful attempts, Miss Ross turned back to Kacy. 'It won't accept this series of numbers, Miss Angelle.' She glanced at the notice again, then turned it over and looked at the back of it. 'I'll bet it's one of his special accounts.' She shrugged her slender shoulders. 'Sorry.'

Exasperation tried to find its way into Kacy's answer, but she fought it back. Trying to get more information from Miss Ross would be tantamount to whipping a dead horse. 'Isn't there anyone else who can help me?'

'I'm afraid not. Unless the data on your loan is available, no one else can tell you any more than I can.'

This can't be happening, Kacy told herself. *It's just some computer foul-up. Don't panic.* 'All right,' she said with more calm than she felt. 'Reschedule my appointment as early as possible on the day he gets back. That'll still give us three weeks to get this mess straightened out.'

Relief registered in Miss Ross's clear blue eyes. 'Done. His morning's full, but I'll put you down for his first appointment after lunch on Monday, December second. That way you won't have to wait long.'

Kacy pulled out her date book and flipped to December second. She would have to reschedule Mandy's dental checkup, but that shouldn't be a problem. 'Fine.' She slipped into her all-weather coat with a quick glance at her watch. There was nothing she could do in the meantime, so she might as well get on with business as usual. She'd have just enough time to pick up the cleaning supplies before making Wee Care's afternoon pickups at the schools.

Alone in the elevator, Kacy had time to rehash what had just happened. *It won't accept this series of numbers.* That would mean that Wee Care's records weren't in the bank's computer. *Private account?* If Miss Ross was right, what was going on?

From nowhere the stranger's words leaped into her head. *Do yourself a favor. Take your business elsewhere.*

A shiver that had nothing to do with the temperature passed through her. There, between floors, the import of his words suddenly became crystal clear: They had been a warning, pure and simple.

★　★　★

It was uncommonly dark for late morning. For the past several weeks thunderclouds had threatened the Texas Gulf Coast, but Dan Wilder didn't notice them any more today than he had before. He slid across the tattered upholstery and inserted the key in the ignition. Almost as an afterthought, he stretched a long jeans-encased leg and checked his pocket for the second set of keys. Satisfied that they were there, he drove from the refinery parking lot, then pulled onto the blacktop road that led to I-10 and back to Houston.

Three weeks had passed since the funeral and his near-disastrous confrontation with Hawkins; three long weeks in which he'd isolated himself from his work and the outside world. The isolation had paid off. His plan was coming together.

He glanced up, catching his reflection in the rearview mirror, and grimaced at the bloodshot eyes staring back at him. The days of planning and sleepless nights at the cabin had taken their toll. Dark circles around his eyes magnified the sallow undertone his skin had taken during his self-imposed seclusion. Of course, the booze hadn't helped much, either.

With a yank, he tugged the Oiler-blue baseball cap lower over his forehead, then checked his reflection with a more critical eye. He'd been long past needing a haircut the day his world had fallen apart; consequently his hair was much longer than he usually wore it. The beard he now sported was dark and thick — just the way he wanted it — and it itched like hell. He scratched his jaw and consoled himself with the knowledge that if all went well, his mission would be accomplished in a few short hours. He could shave tonight and feel and look human again.

A rumble in his belly reminded him that he hadn't eaten a real meal in all the time he'd been gone. Lunch at Waylon's Wagon Wheel would be as good a time as any to test the disguise. If the hair and beard could fool Betty Lou, Waylon's flirtatious new waitress, he would have no trouble getting past the ever-vigilant Miss Ross. If not . . .

His thoughts were sidetracked when he realized he'd almost missed his exit. Minutes later, he maneuvered the unfamiliar vehicle into a parking spot in front of his favorite lunchtime haunt. Before he even reached for the key to cut the engine, his fingers froze on the wheel. Two uniformed officers sat framed in the diner's front window. Ever since Ray's death, Dan knew that his thinking had sometimes been off center. The grief of losing his only brother had left him shaken to the core; his anger that the law had been so tight-lipped about Ray's involvement in their little scheme had made Dan more determined than ever to get at the truth.

But the unexpected presence of Houston's finest forced him to consider the legal aspects of his carefully plotted scheme. The authorities weren't involved in his plan, which meant that, legal or not, anything he turned up would be admissible in court. What he didn't know was whether or not he would be prosecuted for his high-handed method of acquiring the evidence. Would the law again be twisted to protect the criminals, or would justice be served at last?

Lingering only briefly, he killed the engine. Then, with the same resolve that had carried him this far, he stepped from the car and headed for the door. Inside, the cafe was filled with the usual lunch crowd, workmen from various utility companies, a few construction workers killing time until they decided if the weather was going to get better or worse, and a half-dozen or so kids from a nearby high school. He paid scant attention to any of them as he straddled the only vacant stool at the counter.

With nothing more than a half-hearted promise to return for his order, Betty Lou plopped a slick red menu and a glass of water before him. So much for red-hot flirtations, he groused, convinced now that Miss Ross would be no problem. In the mirror behind the counter, he watched the police officers sipping their coffee and talking quietly.

Law and order. Uninvited, the words jumped into his mind.

Good against evil. The muscles along his jawline tensed.

Right versus wrong. His fingers tightened around the amber plastic glass.

19

His brother was dead. The men responsible were free. Something was cockeyed somewhere.

His thoughts raced around and over each other, tugging the ache lurking in the back of his head to the forefront. One of the officers seemed to sense Dan's stare and looked up. Dan nodded politely, and picked up the cup of coffee Betty Lou had slung at him on her last sweep by. The cop hesitated before returning the nod, then turned his attention back to what his partner was saying.

Dan breathed easier, and instantly felt foolish for his paranoia. He was a law-abiding citizen — at least for the moment — and the police had no reason to be suspicious of him. Even so, one thought was ever-present: One way or another, Ray's death would not go unpunished, even if it meant that he had to kill Hawkins himself.

★ ★ ★

Kacy hoped she looked more confident than she felt for her meeting with the man who held the future of Wee Care in the balance. It had been the longest three and a half weeks she'd ever lived through. Especially after she and Mary had gone over the loan agreement. All the financial mumbo jumbo had left them with more questions than answers. Kacy's first impulse had been to call their attorney; Mary had been her optimistic self, saying there was time for that after Kacy talked with Hawkins. Kacy still wasn't convinced.

From the very beginning, she'd had a funny feeling about the loan Hawkins had finally secured for them. Southside had been the first place they went to for financing. Regretfully, Hawkins informed them on that first visit almost five years ago, two divorcees, neither with a past credit history of her own, were poor risks for a loan of the amount they were seeking. They had left disheartened, but still hopeful. It was, after all, an ideal location for a day-care center, and while Kacy held degrees in psychology and business management, Mary had her own in child development. Unfortunately for them, three other lending institutions agreed with Hawkins. Just as they were about to give up, Hawkins called with good news: He'd found an alternative for them.

His offer hadn't been ideal, but it allowed them to start their play school. They'd had to scrounge up twice the amount of money they had saved for a down payment, and the loan interest was four points higher than any of the banks they'd approached. That had been bad enough, but they hadn't counted on *this*.

A low rumble in the sky made Kacy quicken her step. She'd left the van for service at Taylor's Automotive four blocks away. With a little luck she'd make it to the bank before the rain that had threatened all morning came in a downpour. Gulf Coast weather was so unpredictable in the winter. Warm and balmy one day, and bone-chilling cold the next. The past week, she remembered, tucking her chin down into her collar, had been one rainstorm after another. She shoved her hands deep inside the pockets of her jacket and bounded up the four steps to the bank's entrance. The wind picked up and she wished she hadn't left her all-weather coat in the van. Her black linen slacks and jacket were stylish enough, but not even the added warmth of the red turtleneck could keep the early December chill from driving through her.

A gust whipped in from the south, wrapped around her, and hurled her with a force she couldn't withstand into the embrace of a tall, bearded man.

Knocked off balance, Kacy groped for his arms as he reached out to steady her. She finally found her footing and muttered a polite 'Thank you.' Glancing up, she looked straight into the face and green-green eyes she'd had to force out of her thoughts repeatedly over the past three weeks. Only today the face was covered with a thick growth of beard and the eyes were red where they should have been white. A baseball cap covered his long dark hair. His fleece-lined jacket opened to reveal a brown plaid shirt. Dark ropers covered his feet. He looked nothing like the impeccably dressed man who had barged into Hawkins' office three weeks ago. At a glance or at a distance, she never would have recognized him.

'You — ' The look he gave her chopped off the rest of her words. The scowl that pulled his eyebrows together made it clear that he recognized her as well. Her gaze fell to the athletic bag he'd dropped to grab her. It was unzipped and inside she saw bundles of money, lots of money. Then she saw the handgun stuffed in the waistband of his jeans.

Instead of releasing her, his grip tightened, and she looked up to see his eyes narrow to menacing slits. All the pieces suddenly fell into place. She tried to pull free, but he retained his hold, began to drag her along with him toward the curb.

'What — ' Again he silenced her with a look.

Then, with her firmly in tow, he ducked around the corner and pushed her through the driver's door of a mud-brown Pinto. She scrambled for the passenger door, but he was quicker. He grabbed her by the arm and hauled her back. She tried to speak again.

'Be quiet and scoot over.' He sounded more irritated than threatening. 'And don't try anything like that again.' He tossed the gym bag into the back-seat.

'What . . . what are you doing?' Her voice shook with fear. 'What do you want with me?'

The engine sputtered to life on the second try and he turned his head to look her dead in the eye.

'Like it or not, looks like I've got myself a hostage.'

2

Hos . . . tage. Hos . . . tage. The word replayed over and over in Kacy's mind, breaking up in nerve-wracking cadence with the wipers' back-and-forth motion. Rain fell in sheets now, obscuring her view of the street she traveled at least twice a day.

Clutching her handbag to her breast, she'd fought hysteria from the moment she realized the unthinkable had happened: She had been abducted. If she wanted to see Mandy again, she knew she had to remain alert, watch for any opportunity to escape.

Careful to keep her movements slow and unnoticed, she chanced a glance at her captor. He appeared intent on his driving. His booted foot stepped on the brake even as she watched. Hope instantly sprang to life inside Kacy. He was slowing down.

She glanced up toward the front of the car and saw the traffic light ahead turning red. Now, she told herself. *Just take it slow and easy.* The only thing in her favor at this point was that she knew where she was. If she moved fast enough, she could leap from the car, then race for the fire station on the next block. It was her only chance.

She tried to breathe normally while letting her right hand slide unnoticed off her thigh. So far, so good. Next all she had to do was grab the door handle . . .

'Don't even think about it.' He didn't raise his voice. His hands never left the wheel. The engine idled so roughly that Kacy couldn't tell if it was the rattletrap car shaking or her. She swallowed, then looked out the window again. The light was still red; she still had time . . .

'I know it's tempting.' This time the edge of warning in his words made Kacy's mouth go dry. 'But not very smart.' He paused, and Kacy couldn't

27

help looking at him. The storm-darkened sky outside his window cast his profile in a sinister light. 'Even if you make it out the door, who's going to help you?'

Until he called her attention to it, she hadn't noticed the absence of other vehicles on the road. Straight ahead, she saw nothing but an empty street; to her left and her right, the same thing. Obviously any pedestrians unfortunate enough to be out when the storm hit had taken shelter wherever they could. If she didn't make it to the fire station, there wasn't a soul to help her. Her throat constricted, her stomach knotted painfully. Maybe he wouldn't try to stop her once she was out of the car . . .

'I'll just have to chase you down and haul you back,' he said, putting an end to that notion. 'Save us both the trouble.'

If he meant to intimidate her, it wouldn't work. She hadn't survived a year of hell to become another man's victim. She had to take the chance.

Besides, too much was at stake for her to become passive now — Mandy's welfare, Wee Care's future, her own sanity.

With a calculated grab, she pulled the handle and pushed with all her might. Her shoulder banged against the door, but nothing happened. Again she yanked and shoved. Still, nothing. In her panic, it didn't dawn on her that he hadn't tried to stop her. One last frantic search for the door lock and her heart sank. All she found was a broken nub where the stem should have been. For the first time, she looked straight at him. He sat there calmly facing forward, so unconcerned that Kacy had to restrain herself from physically striking out at him.

'Damn you!' More angry now than frightened, she forced back the tears of frustration. He'd known all along that the lock was broken.

The light turned green, and he accelerated toward the maze of freeways looming in the distance. Once he reached the legal speed limit, he kept it steady. His timing seemed perfect. With a growing sense of doom, Kacy watched the traffic lights take turns changing to green as the car approached each one.

It took some doing, but soon her breathing returned to a semblance of normality. This was crazy. She had no idea who he was, had only seen him the one other time. How could she be a threat to him? No sooner had she asked herself the question than it dawned on her. Although she didn't know him by name, she had gathered that Hawkins did. What was the name he'd called out before the door slammed shut? Williams? Wilde? The name escaped her, but all she had to do was tell someone that today's culprit — and it was becoming increasingly apparent that he was indeed a culprit — was the same man who had stormed into Hawkins's office ahead of her three weeks ago. She shook her head, as if to clear her thoughts. Something about that bothered her. Hawkins could just as easily tell the authorities who he was as she could, so that left her right back where she started.

She continued to worry the matter around in her head until she noticed that he'd taken the I-10 East on-ramp. Pre-rush-hour traffic was light, and he took the inside lane with ease. He settled back and gradually picked up speed. At this rate they would be out of Houston soon. She had to do something, but what?

Suddenly she remembered a talk show she'd seen on TV just last week. The host had been interviewing a panel of criminals, which included rapists and kidnappers. The experts were there as well, giving advice on how victims should react to being taken against their will. Where one strongly advocated fighting back, another was just as adamant that any show of resistance would only inflame the aggressor, possibly goad him into more violent

31

action. He was of the opinion that the victim should carefully, calmly try to reason with the captor, try to make him see her as a person with feelings and loved ones, just like him. Even the criminals had disagreed among themselves, leaving the viewer with no real answers.

All Kacy had to go on now was her own personal experience. Neither tactic had worked with Ted. Pleading with him had only added to his enjoyment of tormenting her; fighting back had made him more angry, more intent on carrying through with the beatings.

She glanced at the man sitting beside her, so intent on his driving. She'd tried to escape and it hadn't worked. Remembering how violent he'd been with Hawkins, she decided that reasoning with him was worth a try.

'Look . . . ' she ventured, hesitating when he didn't respond. Encouraged by his silence, she was determined that the fear roiling around inside her would not show in her voice. 'I don't know why you're doing this — '

'Save your breath.' He leaned forward and wiped at the fog on the windshield with his hand. All he got for his effort was a wide smear in his line of vision. He muttered an expletive, then lowered his window an inch or so. In a matter of seconds, the fog began to disappear. The smudge didn't. He wiped at it again, and made matters worse. Under normal circumstances, Kacy might have found this small annoyance funny. But these weren't normal circumstances, and he wasn't just annoyed.

Almost as if to drive the thought home, he suddenly stripped off his cap and slapped it on the seat between them. Her arms jerked up to shield herself from the blow that never landed, a reflex that had lain dormant but alive inside her for years. She closed her eyes tightly, and in that fleeting moment she suffered again every broken bone, every painful bruise. Her pulse raced, she felt light-headed, ill.

'Damn, lady,' he swore. 'I'm not going to hurt you.'

I'm sorry, Kacy. I didn't mean to hurt you. Now that the dam had cracked, she couldn't stop the flood of words from the past. *Please forgive me. It will never happen again.*

'Are you okay?' Just as he had cued the memories, he stopped them by speaking again.

She opened her eyes to see surprise and shock in the stranger's face.

'I'm not going to hurt you,' he repeated softly. He looked like he didn't know what to think. He also looked and sounded sincere. Something in his words and manner soothed her. Still, she wasn't about to simply take him at his word. Frankly she found it difficult to trust a man who would drag an innocent bystander off the street, stuff her in a car, and drive away. The promise she'd kept all these years rang in her ear: *No man will ever hurt me again.*

Still clinging to her handbag, more to

stop the trembling that had come with the memories than anything else, she watched him run his fingers through his hair, heard him draw a deep breath. Suddenly she remembered the look in his eyes that day three weeks ago. She would be a fool not to be afraid, but somehow, in her heart, she knew that he had spoken the truth. He wouldn't hurt her.

So why couldn't she stop shivering? She hugged what little warmth she could to herself and tried to stop her teeth from chattering.

'The heater doesn't work.' She heard the apology in his voice and that was the last either spoke as they continued to travel east on I-10.

She had no way of knowing how far they'd come until they sped past the Houston city limits sign. Alarmed, she searched the unlighted instrument panel for the clock, only to find that it, like the heater, didn't work. The weather had worsened, making the sky unusually dark for early afternoon. The face on her watch was so small that it was impossible to see it in the fading light. She could only guess that they had been on the road for a little less than an hour.

The man beside her reached into his shirt pocket and brought out something red, a piece of paper that he hung on the rearview mirror. His movement drew her attention, and she took her eyes off the road for only a few seconds. But it was enough for her to realize her mistake. She felt the car easing off the freeway, and jerked her eyes back to the road. Too late she saw that he had left the Interstate. Damn, she swore to herself. She'd missed the name of the exit he'd taken.

The longer they traveled, the heavier the rain fell and the darker it grew outside. Finally he pulled onto the shoulder of the two-lane road and killed the engine. Next, he turned off the headlights, and darkness engulfed them. All she could see were the lights clinging to the silhouettes of refinery smokestacks jutting into the sky in the distance.

What would he do now? Since he was safely out of town, would he let her go, or . . . ?

Icy fingers of dread tightened around her throat, almost cutting off her breathing. She'd tried being brave, even tried to escape, but neither had worked. Maybe appealing to his conscience would.

'Please, mister, I have a little girl.' The pleading note in her voice summoned more painful memories, memories of her futile begging —

'Won't work.' This time his eyes settled on her, and even in the gloom of darkness she saw the determination in them. 'Do as I say and you'll be home in a few days.' He didn't give her time to argue. Instead, he reached over and pulled her down into the seat. Panic gripped her, and she struggled against his hold.

'No!' she screamed.

His grip tightened. 'Dammit, lady.

How many times do I have to tell you I'm not going to hurt you?'

She heard the words and tried to believe they were true. But it was as useless as her struggling. It didn't take long to wear herself out. Exhausted, she lay still. His hand rested on her shoulder with just enough pressure to let her know that he would do whatever it took to restrain her.

Unable to see what was happening, Kacy's other senses became acutely alive. The tattered upholstery rubbed abrasively against her cheek; the musty odor made it hard to breathe. She heard cars passing from both directions, many cars. The only reason for the sudden flow of traffic on such a lonely stretch of highway was that they were near a plant or a refinery and that it was time for the shifts to change. As suddenly as the traffic started, it stopped, and, cold and restless, she tried to move.

'Stay put.' He punctuated his order with more pressure. Several long minutes passed, then she felt him lean forward, turn the key in the ignition. He must have used his left hand because the right one remained on her shoulder.

The ancient motor churned, sputtered, and coughed. But it didn't start. Kacy didn't know whether to be relieved or not. He swore softly, then pumped the accelerator three or four times. At last it caught, and he drove a distance before slowing and turning left.

Soon the car came to a stop, and this time he moved his hand to turn off the motor. Kacy sat up, leaving her purse where it had lain beneath her body. She tried to get her bearings while he reached under the seat and pulled out a sheet of cardboard. Scrawled in large black letters were the words DEAD BATTERY. Tossing it onto the dashboard, he grabbed the athletic bag and a black western hat from the backseat. Quickly stuffing the discarded baseball cap into the bag, he tugged the hat low over his forehead.

'Let's go.' His monosyllabic, two-word demands were getting on her nerves, and stubbornly she refused to move. His only response was a shake of his head and a firm grip on her wrist. To hell with what the experts said. She couldn't just go along, like a lamb to the slaughter. She had to do something.

Struggling just enough that he wouldn't notice her stuffing her purse into the crack between the seat and its back, she finally followed him out the door. Long shot that it was, she prayed that someone would find it and —

'I'd have been disappointed if you hadn't tried that,' he said with a wry little grin. She couldn't be sure, but she thought she heard a trace of respect in his voice. Respect or not, it didn't stop him from reaching in and working the bag from its hiding place. He stuffed it into his bag and gave her a grim little smile.

Freed now, she couldn't contain her indignation. 'I'd be so disappointed in myself if I disappointed you.' Her retort made him smile, a slow, easy smile that washed the harshness away from his chiseled features. The combination — the smile, the play of crows-feet at the corner of his eyes, the indentations on each side of his mouth — distracted her momentarily before she made herself look away.

Outside for the first time in over an hour, she took in her surroundings. The significance of the red tag he'd hung on the rearview mirror struck her now. They were in the employees' parking lot of the Tex-Oil Refinery. Only vehicles with the appropriate parking permit were allowed in this area. There wasn't another person in sight. The rain had sent everyone getting off work hurriedly on their way home; everyone coming to work was already inside. That was why he'd waited so long on the side of the road . . . so there would be no one in the parking lot to see them.

'This way.' Strong fingers gripped hers, causing her to wince as he threaded her through the maze of parked cars. Try as she might, it was hard for her to keep up with him. At last he stopped at a black pickup and unlocked the door.

The first thing Kacy saw was the dealer's sticker on the window, and she saw it only because it struck her face-high. And the reason for that was the truck's oversize tires. At first, Kacy resisted the man's hand at her elbow. In the end, she had to accept his help in climbing up into the cab. He tossed the bag onto the floorboard at her feet, then climbed in beside her. Unlike the junkheap they'd just abandoned, the truck was brand-new clean, inside and out, and it started on the first try. Slowly they drove past the security booth and onto the road again. With a sinking heart, Kacy wedged her body against the door. The more the storm intensified, the darker it became, leaving Kacy filled with a sense of foreboding that grew stronger with each mile and minute that passed.

Dan Wilder tried not to let the frightened woman wedged against the far door see how disturbed he was. He wasn't a man without conscience, and now that he'd had time to think, he regretted having involved her in this mess. And what a mess it was. Things hadn't gone exactly as planned, and *that* was an understatement.

Until Miss Ross had blundered in and seen him holding Hawkins at gunpoint, he'd held the advantage. From that point on, it had been a disaster. She might be young and inexperienced, but she'd seen enough to *think* that Hawkins was being robbed. All the evidence had been right there in plain sight: the open safe, the gun, the money, the bag that already had the computer disks inside. His only break had been that Miss Ross hadn't recognized him. To protect himself, Hawkins would have to go along with Miss Ross's eyewitness account. As senior loan officer, he could easily replace the twenty-five thousand dollars Dan had taken from his ill-gotten office cache with bank money, lending credence to the robbery scenario later when the discrepancy was verified. No doubt Hawkins would keep his mouth shut concerning the identity of the thief. They both had too much to lose if the law knew who they were looking for at this stage of the game. Dan now had the evidence Ray had died trying to get; Hawkins wouldn't want to be linked in any way to Ray's death.

But his luck ran out on the steps in front of the bank. He had recognized her immediately, and the look on her face had told him she'd seen past the hair and the beard. Until the moment he forced her to come with him, he hadn't committed any real crime. But kidnapping — now that was a different thing altogether. If only he hadn't spoken to her that day he'd come so close to killing Hawkins; if only she hadn't recognized him today; if only

Ray had been able to come to him instead . . .

Dammit! Stop what-iffing. It would change nothing, and at the moment he needed to concentrate on keeping his . . . his victim — there was no other word for it — calm. Silently he swore again. Then he looked at her. Dark hair framed a face that was pale and drawn; her small chin quivered, and when she saw him looking at her, she turned away defiantly. But not before he saw the fear that he had put in her dark eyes.

Something akin to regret gnawed at his insides. Even in the agitated state of mind he'd been in that first time he'd seen her, he had felt something he never thought he'd feel again. But this wasn't the time for personal regrets, he reproached himself.

Lowering the window and tossing out the keys to the clunker he'd paid cash for earlier that morning, he changed his train of thought. As soon as Hawkins had the chance, he'd get word to his cronies and they'd be after him. They'd been on to Ray and Michaelson's plan from the beginning, probably knew that Dan was going to turn the disks over to Michaelson. By being at the wrong place at the wrong time, the woman had put herself in jeopardy, and, like it or not, he had to see to it that nothing happened to her. The camp was the best place for her until things cooled off.

To his right, he heard her sigh deeply, saw her draw her coat tighter around herself. What was wrong with him? Scared and wet, she had to be freezing.

Quickly punching buttons on the console, he said, 'Won't take long for it to heat up.'

She stiffened her back to him in answer, and continued to look out the window.

'That's gratitude for you,' he mumbled under his breath. He felt her glare on him in the moment that followed.

'Bank robber, kidnapper, smart ass — all rolled into one nice, neat

46

package,' she countered.

He couldn't help looking at her in wonder. 'Cute. I'm glad to have the fighter back.'

Her dark eyes narrowed. 'Fighter? You ain't seen nothing yet.'

This time he laughed out loud. She turned away with a very unladylike snort, and he had no doubt that she was plotting her next move. That was good. He could deal with a woman determined to take care of herself. He was glad she wasn't a wimp.

'Buckle up,' he told her. If she tried the out-the-door stunt again, she'd have to contend with the seat belt first.

The rain continued to fall in driving sheets. The silence that filled the cab became oppressive, unbearable. During the past three weeks, he'd had enough silence to last a lifetime.

'Divorced?'

'What?' Obviously she'd been engrossed in her own thoughts, thoughts he had no doubt centered on getting away from him.

He inclined his head toward the left hand lying in her lap. 'No ring. And you mentioned that you have a little girl.' Maybe talking would help her relax. How was she to know that he wasn't the villain he appeared to be? For all she knew, he *could be* a bank robber, a serial killer who preyed on loan officers, even a deranged rapist. So far, all she'd seen of him was his foul temper and his strong-arm reactions to her recognizing him.

'Oh,' she answered softly. 'Yes, I'm divorced.'

'There's a lot of that going around.' He tried to smile, to lighten the mood. Somehow he wasn't surprised that it didn't work.

She looked at him with the biggest, brownest eyes he could remember ever seeing. 'You're not going to let me go.' The unqualified conviction in her voice caught him off guard.

He wanted to tell her yes, that he'd let her go when the time was right, that he hadn't wanted to take her in the first place. But he wasn't about to promise something he might not be able to deliver, so he said nothing. Her eyes never left his face. He saw in them a battle between fear and the determination to survive.

Suddenly her chin jutted out in a show of defiance. 'You *said* you'd let me go in a few days.'

He wasn't sure what she had on her mind, but it was definitely something. 'If everything goes the way I want it to.'

'Mandy's going to be alone and frightened.' Her voice was strong, but oddly resigned. She looked small and vulnerable sitting there with her head bowed, her fingers fidgeting in her lap. 'I need to make arrangements for someone to take care of her for me.' She was serious. He was amazed. So far, she'd been one surprise after another.

He'd done some pretty stupid things lately, but even considering this was worse than stupid. It could be deadly.

He couldn't believe that he didn't simply say no.

'I'll stop in Baytown.' He cut his eyes at her. 'If you make one wrong move . . . '

'I won't,' she answered quickly. 'I promise.' She looked relieved but didn't do a very good job of hiding the shudder that overtook her.

Twenty minutes later, he turned into a Texaco station and stopped directly in front of a bank of telephones near the rear of the building. The area was well lit, and a perfect place for her to try to make another getaway attempt. Again, he let her out his side of the truck, all the while keeping his hand at her elbow. She was as good as her word. She didn't make a move that could be construed as threatening.

'My . . . money's in my purse.' She picked up the handset. 'I could call collect.'

He dug into his pocket and turned up roughly two dollars in nickels, dimes, and quarters. 'Nice try,' he said, holding out his hand. She glowered up at him, took a quarter, deposited it, and punched in the numbers.

'Thank you,' she said to the operator, then took more coins and deposited them. 'Mary, it's Kacy.' She paused, listened, then said, 'I know I didn't make the after-school pickup. I'm sorry. The van's still at Taylor's. Please, just listen, Mary. I don't have much time. I've — '

He stepped closer, and her words stopped. She looked up at him. 'I have to go away for a few days. Will you watch Mandy for me?' Another pause. 'Don't press me for details. I can't — '

Dan put his hand over the mouth-piece. 'Tell her you have to go.'

She didn't argue. 'Mary, I have to go now.' She sniffed back the tears he saw welling up in her eyes. He tried to take the phone from her, but she snatched it back. 'I almost forgot . . . ' she added, quickly placing her body between him and the phone. 'Mandy has an appointment at the dentist tomorrow at three-thirty.' Her voice cracked, and she cleared her throat. 'Tell her I love her.' She didn't wait for him to take the receiver away from her this time. She hung up on her own.

Dan had experienced every emotion possible in the past few weeks, but this was a new one. He felt like slime. A month ago he wouldn't have thought himself capable of holding a man at gun point, tying him and a frightened young woman together in a corner, then forcing an innocent bystander into his car simply because she had recognized him. But keeping a mother away from her child was an all-time low. Grief and anger had a way of working together to make a man do desperate things.

Taking the woman — whose name he now knew was Kacy — by the arm, he helped her back into his truck. She scooted quickly to her side of the cab to sit in resigned silence, or so it appeared. He'd seen enough to know that she wasn't one to give up entirely. He'd have to watch her closely. He motioned for her to buckle her seat belt. Knowing that her little girl would be taken care of should comfort her to a small degree. At least he hoped so. Maybe a little easy-listening music would help, too.

He fumbled through the built-in cassette case in the dash, then took out one of his favorite tapes and plugged it into the player. In a matter of seconds, Henry Mancini's rendition of country music filled the cab.

Dan leaned back and tried to relax. They were in for a long night. He admired her spunk, but he was too tired to put up with a strong-willed woman. Maybe once they were at the cabin, she would realize the hopelessness of trying to escape.

3

Years of being on her own had made Kacy Angelle a practical woman, which was the only reason she hadn't fallen to pieces. She had to be alert for any chance of escape. For the moment she'd decided against doing anything that might draw attention to herself. Every time he looked at her, it either brought back things she'd rather not remember or it made her pulse go all haywire. Either way, he muddled her thinking, and she had to think clearly to survive this ordeal and go home to her little girl.

Her little girl. Kacy closed her eyes to shut out the dismal blending of gray asphalt and rain splattering against the windows. Practical or not, she was suddenly very tired, so tired that in spite of her anxiety, the music flowing from the speakers eventually had a calming effect. She drew a deep breath and allowed her mind to wander back to the day Mandy had come into her life. Houston's Hobby Airport had been bustling with Christmas travelers, and it had taken longer than Kacy planned to find the gate for the plane arriving from Dallas. At the age of four, the child had looked so tiny and alone, so frightened and deserted that it had taken every ounce of Kacy's willpower to keep from smothering her with the love that had immediately overwhelmed her. How could anyone *not* want such a perfectly beautiful little girl?

As a teen Connie had always been flighty and self-centered, Kacy recalled. As a woman, her cousin had become nothing short of irresponsible and selfish. No matter how badly Kacy wanted children, she'd had reservations about taking on Connie's cast-off child. Now, two years later, she couldn't imagine life without her. In a few short months the adoption would be final, if —

She cut off the negative thought. *When* she and Mandy stood before the judge, the child would legally become Amanda Brooke Angelle. Kacy still couldn't believe that Connie had agreed to the adoption — and all in a casual, long-distance telephone conversation that had taken less than three minutes.

'I could use some coffee and a bite to eat . . . ' The man's voice intruded on her thoughts. 'How about you?'

Kacy had been so caught up in her mental driftings, she hadn't noticed that darkness had finally fallen. She glanced up to see the lights of Beaumont twinkling a welcome in the near distance. The thought of food made her ill, but as long as they were moving, there was no way she could get away. Not trusting her voice to conceal her line of thought, she gave him a quick, decisive nod.

'Good.' His eyes never left the road. 'Now, scoot over here next to me, and — '

'I know,' Kacy interrupted with as much contempt as she dared. 'Buckle up.' Damn him, he was one step ahead of her, and he wasn't taking any chances. She released the harness strap that held her firmly in place, slid across the seat, and wrapped the middle seat belt around her.

The cab had seemed small and confined before, but now that she sat so close that their thighs touched, she was conscious of nothing but him. The way his hands gripped the steering wheel, the tense set of his angular jaw, the smell of his damp clothes. She inhaled the scent of outdoors and wind and smoke, not that of tobacco but of a fireplace or a campfire. All in all, a smell that lulled her into a sense of security that was completely at odds with her circumstances. She couldn't remember ever feeling so safe, so protected.

Protected? Realizing what a crazy path her poor, befuddled brain had taken, she had to forcefully subdue the urge to return to the relative safety of her corner.

Minutes later, they pulled away from McDonald's drive-through window with two bags sitting in Kacy's lap. Much to Kacy's consternation, he hadn't even killed the engine, much less thought about going inside. She sat quietly plotting her next move.

'Mind handing me one of those burgers?' he asked. 'And coffee.' He had his hands full getting back on I-10 and fighting the bumper-to-bumper traffic created by the storm and road construction.

Kacy opened one of the boxes, wrapped a napkin around the burger, and handed it to him. 'I . . . ' Her thoughts went askew when his hand wrapped around hers by mistake. He finally took hold of the burger, then looked at her. 'I have to go . . . you know . . . to the restroom.' Why hadn't she thought of that sooner?

His brow creased, and she knew he recognized the request for exactly what it was — another ploy for escape.

'I'll see what I can do,' he answered, and Kacy knew she hadn't imagined the unspoken 'Yeah, sure.'

She'd have been in trouble if she'd really needed to relieve herself. He passed every freeway exit without a second glance, then they were on the open road again.

Irked by his callous disregard to her request, Kacy made a production of scooting back to her side of the cab. 'Thanks for trying, but I can wait.' She didn't have to try for sarcasm. It found its way into her voice naturally. He smiled around a bite of burger. Again, she put her back to him and stared out the window. Droplets of water twisted and turned in tracks patterned by the wind on the outside of the glass. Their erratic dances kept her mind occupied until her eyes closed and, in spite of her resolve, she dozed off.

A flash of lightning and clap of thunder jerked her awake some time later. She blinked away the sleep and sat up. They were no longer on the Interstate, and no other cars were in sight. The two-lane country road they traveled now was deserted, except for the pine trees and foliage hugging the fenceline that ran along with them for miles. Disoriented, she had no idea if they were still traveling east — or had he turned north, perhaps south? Time dragged by, and the headlights picked up a flash of white in the distance. Kacy strained to see, focused intently on the road sign that grew larger as they moved nearer. She sucked in her breath as the letters became distinguishable, formed words. Sabine River.

The hollow echo of the wheels crossing the bridge roared in her ears, and, unfamiliar though she was with the area, she knew that once they crossed the Sabine, they were no longer in Texas. They had entered Louisiana.

Silently she cursed herself for falling asleep. How many chances had she missed to get away? And how much farther did he plan to go?

Almost in answer to her last question, the truck slowed, crossed the center line, then eased off the left shoulder of the road.

Kacy leaned forward, dumbstruck, and stared through the rain-splattered windshield. The waters of the rain-swollen Sabine lapped at the front bumper.

The man was crazy. He couldn't actually intend to keep going. For as far as she could see there was no road, no trail, just acres of flooded bottom land.

Frantic, she grabbed for the steering wheel. The shoulder strap dug into her shoulder, stopping her from doing any real damage. 'What are you doing?' she asked in fright.

The truck lurched to a stop less than a foot from the trunk of a massive cypress tree. He shook her off with a scowl that sent her back to her corner. All she could do was huddle against the door and watch him press a button on the armrest console. Her window lowered just over halfway. Wind and rain swirled into the cab, adding to the chill that gripped her.

'Grab that,' he ordered, nodding his head toward the open window. A strip of cloth tied to a low-hanging branch danced in the wind, almost hitting her in the face. She tugged it loose, and the window went up. She didn't know what to do with the wet rag, so she clutched it tightly in her hand. In the faint glow from the instrument panel, Kacy saw his eyes scanning the trees in front of them. Finally he saw whatever it was that he was searching for. Angling toward nowhere as far as Kacy could tell, he moved on, then stopped again, lowered the window, and pointed out another piece of torn fabric. No sooner did she catch it than the window went up, and he gunned the engine.

They continued through the woods and backwater for over an hour, taking down trail markers along the way. Visibility wavered between poor and nonexistent, their progress slow and tedious.

In the total darkness that surrounded them, the headlights bathed everything in their path in bouncing light, casting each massive oak, every Spanish moss-laden cypress as a demon lying in wait. Kacy was numb with disbelief, which had to account for her uncharacteristic willingness to do whatever he told her. The closest she had ever come to venturing into the wilds was an occasional Wee Care excursion to Hermann Park Zoo.

Suddenly she felt the truck lose momentum, heard the tires whirling in the mud.

'Damn.'

Kacy jumped at the first word either had spoken in over an hour.

'Don't get stuck on me now.' His words were both a threat and a plea. His expression hardened in concentration as he shifted into reverse, then back into drive. Over and over, he repeated this process, rocking the vehicle back and forth until it finally broke free of the mire that had threatened to trap them.

Kacy released a sigh, realizing as she did that she had been pulling for *him*. They plowed on through rain and mud, deeper and deeper into the darkness of trees and thicket, farther and farther from the road and civilization.

Finally he killed the engine and turned off the lights. Absolute darkness engulfed them, and she stifled the gasp that threatened to escape her lips. She had known since the beginning that they would have to stop eventually, but she wasn't prepared for it now.

She heard him fumbling around beside her, then he opened his door. The overhead dome light flooded the cab with glaring brightness. Without a word, he reached up and pulled the Tex-Oil parking permit she hadn't noticed before from the rearview mirror. Working quietly, he scooped up the trail marks that cluttered the floor and stuffed them, along with the parking permit and the McDonald's remnants, into a brown paper bag that had appeared from nowhere. Reflexively she drew back when he leaned over and opened the glove compartment. He took a flashlight out, then slammed it shut.

'This is as far as the truck can go.' One deft movement of his thumb and both doors were locked. 'Out this side, and be careful. The underbrush is thick here.' She heard his boots hit water, and she couldn't move.

'I'm not getting out of this truck.' She was adamant.

He didn't seem surprised or angry, and her woman's intuition warned her that wasn't a good sign.

'Have it your way,' he told her, stuffing the keys into his pocket. 'It's only about eight miles back to the road. If you're lucky, you *might* find your way out without the trail markers.' He rubbed his whiskered jaw in thought. 'Now if there was a moon, I'd give you better odds.' He didn't have to tell her what her chances were without the markers or light, but she was willing to take even the slimmest one. She reached for the door handle.

'Then there are the 'gators,' he said, almost casually. 'Not to mention the quicksand and snakes.'

Her hand hovered over the door handle as she glanced over at him. Somehow standing there in the warm glow of the light, he didn't look nearly as ominous as before — or as deadly as alligators or quicksand or snakes. He dragged the bag out, then turned away.

'Wait!' she called, working frantically to free herself of her shoulder harness, then scampering across the seat and out the open door. 'Don't you dare leave me alone.' Both feet sank ankle-deep in mud while water hit her knee-high. She lost both shoes with her first two steps, and knew it was useless to try to find them. Barefoot now, she sloshed awkwardly after him. If it hadn't been for the flashlight's beam, she knew she never would have found him.

At least he didn't give her a hard time. She'd bet he was smiling, though, as his hand wrapped around hers and he led her a short distance.

'Hold this,' he said, handing her the flashlight. She did as he told her, and watched in quiet confusion while he tore away at the pile of limbs and brush before them.

He worked hard and fast, and Kacy's heart swelled with horror at the sight of the canoe he uncovered.

'Oh, no.' She shook her head, backed up a clumsy step or two. 'I can't get in that thing.'

Long, hard fingers curled around her arm, applied just enough pressure to quiet her. 'We only have a few miles to go.'

'No,' Kacy all but whimpered. 'You don't understand. I can't swim.'

Even in the darkness, she saw his features soften. 'I wish I had time to coax you, Kacy, but I don't.' She heard the exasperation and the weariness in his voice, but it was the way he said her name that cut through her hysteria.

'Now, it's either me and this canoe,

or you and the slough.' He reached out and lifted her chin. Taken unaware by his unexpected gentleness, all she could do was return his gaze. 'Believe me, you're a hundred percent better off with me than you would be alone.' He waited for his words to sink in, then he handed her the only boat cushion in sight. A heavy stream of rainwater rolled off his hat brim. 'Now, move to the middle of the canoe, put the cushion on the bottom, and sit on it. You'll be okay.' He gave her hand a gentle squeeze.

She must be in shock, she thought numbly. Why else would she simply do as he told her? Why else, indeed. She had no choice.

Moments later, settled in the canoe as he'd instructed, she listened to the methodical sounds of the paddle slapping water behind her, easing them steadily through the night and rain. She tried not to think about the small boat or where they were going. Or that, like it or not, her survival depended on two things: her own strength to endure whatever lay ahead — and the disquieting stranger responsible for her being here.

★ ★ ★

Dan hated complications. Always had. They complicated things. He could handle the weather, he could handle the canoe and the river. He knew this slough like it was the equipment yard of Wilder Construction. Every road, paved or dirt, that led to the cabin was flooded. The fact that the bottom was under several feet of water was an inconvenience that happened once or twice a year, but it didn't really bother him. He would find his way to the cabin. The real problem was the woman.

She hadn't said another word after he'd talked her into the boat. She sat there where he'd told her, huddled up and so still that he wanted to shake the fight back into her. He hadn't been surprised when she refused to get out of the truck. Hell, he'd expected it. But the canoe had been her undoing. If he could, he'd have packed her back in the truck right then and there and returned her to her nice safe home. But how safe would she really be until Hawkins and his syndicate were under lock and key?

He shook the thought away with another expletive. What the hell was the matter with him? He'd gone too far now to go soft just because her doe-brown eyes pleaded with him every time she looked at him.

He smiled at that. He'd wager she'd die if she knew the signals those eyes gave out. She was holding up better than any other woman would have; she fought him at every turn, defied him with biting comebacks whenever she could. The only time she'd come close to cowing had been when he lost his patience with the foggy windshield. He hadn't given her cause to think that he had any plans to physically harm her, but she had jerked her arms up to ward off a blow. What had made her react like that?

Stop it! he commanded himself, slamming the paddle into the water. Her problems weren't his. He had enough of his own. His best bet was to keep her angry at him. He could deal with her hostility. He remembered how he'd felt the two times her vulnerability had surfaced unexpectedly. God help him if she ever fell apart on him.

Rain continued to fall; the wind kicked up from the north. The combination of cold north winds and water made him appreciate the felt hat and the fleece-lined jacket he wore.

Again his eyes sought her hunched-over figure through the mizzly rain. She had to be freezing. Her coat, a stylish jacket of some flimsy fabric he couldn't call by name, was soaked through and through. He stopped paddling long enough to take the cap from the gym bag. Careful not to rock the canoe unduly, he eased forward to her.

'Put this on,' he said, having to yell

71

above the wind and rain. She didn't react, nor did she fight him when he placed the cap on her head. Carefully removing his coat, he wrapped it around her shivering shoulders. The flannel shirt he wore was dry, but it wouldn't be for long. He took his seat and began paddling with renewed vigor. The cabin couldn't be more than an hour away.

* * *

Special Agent Hugo Michaelson studied the man behind the desk with contempt. 'I'm not exactly sure what happened here today, Hawkins, but you can bet your ass I'm going to find out.'

Hawkins glared back. 'Why don't you get off my case? I'm the victim here, not the suspect.' He checked his watch. 'Now if you'll excuse me, I have a family waiting for me at home.'

Michaelson gave the banker a smile he knew bordered on being a smirk, pulled up a chair, and folded his lanky frame into it. He didn't doubt for an instant there was a family waiting for him, but its name wasn't Hawkins. 'This won't take long.' He stretched his long legs, crossed them at the ankles, and smiled. 'Now, one more time, from the top.' The son of a bitch was sweating bullets, and that gave Michaelson a great deal of satisfaction. Hawkins was going to have a hard time explaining to his 'family' why he'd drawn so much unwanted attention so soon after the Wilder incident.

Not for the first time in the past few weeks, Michaelson's gut twisted with regret. After eight years with the FBI's Financial Fraud Division, he'd thought that absolutely nothing could get to him anymore. But Ray Wilder's death was something he hadn't counted on, something he'd have to live with for the rest of his life.

Michaelson rested both elbows on the chair arms and laced his fingers together under his chin. Hawkins tried to return his glare, but failed miserably.

The thin sliver of a mustache the banker sported irritated Michaelson no end. To him it represented a sorry attempt to look macho by a sorry excuse of a man. It missed the mark by miles, made him look like a sleazy cartoon ferret slithering around behind his desk. Besides, the bastard was the reason a good man was dead and why Michaelson wasn't sleeping nights.

Which brought him to the reason he was here. Normally he wouldn't have interfered in someone else's routine investigation of a bank robbery, but news travels fast in the Bureau. The minute he'd learned that Hawkins was involved in this one, he'd had a gut feeling he'd be called in on it sooner or later. Michaelson wasn't sure what was going down, but that had never stopped him before.

'We've been over it four times now,' Hawkins complained. 'And there's nothing else to tell.'

'Maybe not.' Michaelson didn't bother to cover his bored yawn or the baiting grin that crept across his face. 'But until your story and Miss Ross's mesh, we'll keep at it.'

A new line of perspiration popped out on Hawkins's forehead. Sometimes Michaelson loved his job.

Behind him, a uniformed officer stuck his head inside the door. 'Excuse me, Detective Michaelson.' He didn't step into the room until the detective motioned for him to do so. 'There's a woman out here demanding to see someone in charge.'

Irritated at being disturbed, Michaelson barked, 'Can't it wait?'

The officer didn't take offense. 'She's pretty upset,' he went on to explain. 'Said something about her friend leaving her van at a garage down the street while she walked to the bank.'

'And?' Michaelson prodded.

'She never picked up her van, and she called later to say she didn't know when she'd be home. Sounded fishy to her friend.' The officer cleared his throat. 'And, sir, this all happened about the same time the suspect was making his getaway.'

Michaelson felt his forehead wrinkle. He pulled his legs back under him with the hope that this was a break and not a complication. Hawkins forgotten for the moment, he stood and strode toward the officer. He turned at the door to face Hawkins one last time.

'Just so there's no misunderstanding, Hawkins . . . ' He paused, wanting the banker to sweat a little more before he left. 'I'm not through with you. Not by a long shot.'

4

Crouched on the floor of the canoe, Kacy shivered against the dank chill that had settled about her like a shroud of despair. Her knuckles felt strained. Her fingers were cramped and sore from clutching the straps of the boat cushion for so long. The man behind her hadn't spoken since placing his coat around her shoulders. She was grateful for his silence, grateful that he focused his attention on maneuvering the small craft broadside with the riverbank. The boat rocked back and forth and she knew without looking that he had stood and leaped ashore. They had reached their destination.

She also knew that she couldn't cower in the bottom of the boat forever, but she was too numb with cold and fear to move on her own. At last, he approached her and extended one hand. Stubbornly she refused his offer of help and tried to stand alone. She stumbled, causing the canoe to totter precariously, and, more afraid of spilling over into the river than of him, she begrudgingly took his proffered hand.

Safely on land at last, Kacy had no choice but to follow him through the storm that gave no sign of letting up. The cap wobbled around on her head, then flew off before she could grab it with her free hand. Dimly it registered on her that they were running up a steep incline. Her legs were about to give out on her when he slowed his pace, giving her a chance to get her wind.

Suddenly a cabin loomed before them in the darkness, and together they mounted the steps to stand on the covered porch in front of the door. He dropped the bag he'd hauled from the canoe and dug in his pocket for his keys. She was so thankful for the shelter that she barely noticed the iron gate that creaked open before he unlocked the wooden entry door.

Inside, it was dark and cold. The door closed behind them with a sound thud and Kacy heard the man stumbling away from her. Lightning flashed outside; thunder rumbled over and over itself. Kacy shrank deeper into the oversize coat. The situation was ominous enough without the added drama of visual and sound effects.

'Damn.' His half-whispered oath echoed from across the room. Kacy backed away until the wall foiled her retreat. More fumbling noises, then a click, and a lamp glowed brightly. She blinked against the light to see him standing near a brown leather recliner.

'Never can remember where that damned table is,' he mumbled, rubbing his shin. They were the first words either had spoken in hours and he seemed as ill at ease as she felt.

Kacy heard her teeth chatter in answer, saw his forehead wrinkle beneath the dripping-wet brim of his cowboy hat.

He tossed the keys next to the lamp on the table. 'Better get out of those wet things.' He turned to the wood bin next to the hearth, then began laying a fire in the stone fireplace.

Kacy knew he was right. She'd been fighting a cold all week and had to get out of her wet clothes. Still, she balked at the idea. She tried to ignore the dread that started to gnaw at her stomach by glancing around her surroundings.

The entire cabin consisted of one large room — very rustic but comfortable enough. To her left and along the opposite wall, beneath a double window, she saw a long, overstuffed sofa. Foot lockers at each end served as tables. The kitchen, a small area located toward the rear of the room, was separated from the living area by an island worktable. Lined along the den side of the long bar were four stools. A half full bottle of Wild Turkey stood on the bar next to an empty glass. The only other door in the cabin, she noted with alarm, led to what looked to be the bathroom.

He stoked the fire to a blaze. 'It'll warm up in a few minutes.' He stood and took a step toward her. 'Let me have my coat — '

Kacy tried to retreat, but forgot that the wall was right behind her.

He stopped immediately. ' — And I'll give you some privacy and get more wood from outside.'

The fleece-lined coat felt as if it weighed fifty pounds and she gladly divested herself of its burden. Apparently satisfied that he wouldn't have to fight her for the garment, he waited while she draped it over the back of the recliner and sidled closer to the fire. The blaze warmed her backside as she watched him rummage through one of the trunks on the other side of the room.

'These'll have to do till your things

dry out.' He tossed what looked like a pair of long johns in her direction. They fell short and landed on the floor in front of her. 'Bathroom's just off the kitchen.' He reached for his coat, pulling it on as he opened the door. Cold, wet air whipped in from outside, and he turned to fix her with a warning scowl. 'I didn't take the scenic route for the exercise,' he said, his voice a flat monotone. 'We're more than ten miles from nowhere, in the middle of a bottom that's surrounded by swamps and marshes.' The dark hat cast a shadow across his rugged features. 'Even when the weather's good, it's hard to get here, but after all this rain, there's no way in or out by land.' Somewhere in the distance an animal howled, a long, haunting cry that underscored his warning.

Without realizing it, Kacy had inched closer to the fire. The scent of scorching fabric reached her nostrils, but she couldn't move.

'You catch my meaning?' He waited

for her to answer. All she could do was nod.

'Good.'

The instant the door closed, Kacy stepped away from the fire. She wasn't stupid, she grumbled to herself. Of course she caught his meaning. She hadn't the faintest idea where she was. It was dark and stormy outside, and she had no desire to brave the river on her own, take the chance of leaving Mandy with no one except Connie to look after her. Escape was impossible. For the moment. Which meant that they would be spending the night alone in this secluded cabin.

Briskly rubbing the backs of her legs, she glanced around the room again, this time with a purpose. So far he'd done nothing to make her think he'd hurt her, but she'd feel better with a weapon. A gun or a knife, anything to help her protect herself.

She had no idea how long he'd be, but she had to act fast. Scurrying across the room, she searched each foot locker thoroughly. All she found in one was men's clothing, shirts, underwear, and jeans; in the other, clean sheets and a couple of extra pillows. The bookshelves that flanked the fireplace were next, but turned up nothing but record albums, audio tapes, and books. Nothing in the drawer of the end table next to the recliner except papers, maps, and bullets . . . a variety of shells of every caliber. Which meant there had to be guns. But where? The only one she recalled was the hand gun tucked snugly in his belt. And she didn't think she was up to taking it away from him — not while he was awake, at least.

Her heart hammered wildly as she glanced around the room again. From its overall appearance, the cabin was a hunter's hideaway, a place where a man could get away from the pressures of everyday life. Surely there were guns stored somewhere. No sooner did the thought occur to her than a cabinet standing in the darkened corner across the way caught her eye. It was huge, made of sturdy cypress and fitted with brass hinges and a lock impressive enough to discourage anyone less desperate than Kacy. Pulling at the doors, she finally had to admit defeat. They simply would not open.

Then she remembered his keys. They were exactly where he'd tossed them earlier, lying on the lamp table.

Her fingers trembled and she swore beneath her breath when the third key she tried failed to open the lock.

Calm down.

She took a deep breath and tried the next key. It slid into the lock with ease. She said a silent prayer of thanks and gave it a turn. Lightning flashed, and she screamed and jumped back. Her gaze flew to the window between the cabinet and the door. She blinked in dismay. Surely her imagination was playing tricks on her. Another flash and her breath lodged in her throat. Bars. There were bars covering every window.

The door flew open and Kacy

swallowed another scream. He loomed in the doorway, his arms laden with firewood. She snatched the keys from the cabinet door, but it was too late. He had already seen them. Kacy expected him to be angry, but he calmly strode to the wood bin and dumped the wood. Then, without a word, he crossed over to her and held out his hand. Like a disobedient child, she ignored the gesture and stubbornly backed away.

His eyebrows pulled together, furrowing his forehead. Then he pulled the hand gun from his belt. For a moment, she thought that she'd finally pushed him too far. To her relief, all he did was take the keys from her, open the cabinet, put the pistol inside, then lock it away.

'I admire your spunk,' he said, quickly locking both the outer gate and the entry door. He stuffed the keys in his pocket and faced her again. 'I thought you understood — '

'No,' Kacy interrupted, willing some mettle into her voice. '*You* don't understand. I won't just sit back and wait for you to decide what you're going to do with me.'

Something akin to admiration flickered in his keen green eyes. 'I take it that means I'll have to keep a closer eye on you.' His lips turned up in a grin so full of devilment that she felt her face flush red. 'Which means no privacy for either of us.' She knew that he was baiting her and she wasn't biting. 'Or,' he went on, 'I could make it easy on myself and tie you up and throw you in a corner.'

This time Kacy felt the color drain from her face. 'You wouldn't dare,' she whispered. The thought of a man physically overpowering her was more than she could endure. He took a step toward her; she took one back. Mercifully he stopped.

'I don't have a lot of options, Kacy.' He kept his distance, but the look in his eyes told her he'd do whatever it took to keep her in line. 'Now, get out of those clothes and into the shower. If you're not through in ten minutes, you'll have to make room for me.'

For the first time, Kacy realized that he was as wet and cold as she was. Beneath his coat, his flannel shirt clung to his chest. His jeans were soaked and muddy. Some tiny worry wart inside her brain wondered if outlaws were meaner and more unreasonable when they were cold and wet. He had yet to raise his voice, but she knew that he was tired, obviously desperate, and for all she knew he might become hostile at any time. She'd be crazy to challenge him.

Besides, all the tension of the day had worn her out. She was too tired to fight him any more tonight. Although she wasn't about to let her guard down, a long, hot bath sounded pretty good. She sidestepped him with a scowl that rivaled his, but without further argument. After switching on the light, the first thing she did was check the door for a lock. She should have known there wouldn't be one.

Leaning against the door, she gave the room a quick once-over. It was nothing out of the ordinary. A small space heater, a lavatory, a toilet, a tub with a shower. It was clean and smelled of pine. Suddenly she felt very tired and very dirty.

Remembering his ten-minute time limit, she was in and out of the shower in record time. Afterward, she wrapped a towel around her body, threw her muddy things into the tub and gave them a quick but thorough washing. It would take more than hand soap to bring life back to the once-chic slacks and matching jacket. The black linen fabric would be stiff and uncomfortable until it was laundered properly. What a time to think about something as everyday as doing the laundry, she thought, tossing her sweater over the shower curtain rod next to her bra and panties. Black, lacy, and undeniably feminine, her underwear had never seemed so provocative as it did hanging in plain view in a stranger's bathroom.

A quick rearrangement of things and the wisps of black lace were carefully concealed under the sweater.

That taken care of, she found that she was faced with an even bigger dilemma. She'd forgotten her change of clothes. A quick search of the bathroom turned up shaving gear, a green container of abrasive cleanser, a bottle of pine oil, a first-aid kit, and nothing larger than the towel she already had wrapped around her body.

How could she have been so careless? As she saw it, she had two choices: She could waltz out there in nothing but a towel and her dignity and retrieve the long johns, or she could have him bring them to her. Considering the circumstances, asking for his help seemed the smarter of the two.

Angry that she'd been so careless, she cracked the door and called out, 'Hey — ' She didn't even know his name. All she heard was the crackling from the fireplace. 'Are you there?' she called again, this time more loudly. Still no answer. He must be getting more wood, she thought, and that narrowed her choices for her. She'd have to get them herself — and before he returned.

Taking care that her towel was securely in place, she eased the door open wider. First she saw her purse lying on the kitchen bar, then her foot stepped on something soft and dry. The long johns lay in a tidy heap in front of the bathroom door. They hadn't walked across the room all by themselves, which left only one way they could have gotten there.

The man who had abducted her was becoming more of an enigma with each moment that passed.

★ ★ ★

Dan took the steps for the fourth time since leaving Kacy to her bath. The wood bin inside now contained enough wood to last through the night; what he'd stacked on the porch would carry her through while he was gone

91

tomorrow. He grumbled an expletive at the top of the landing and rearranged the wood in his arms so he could dig for the key again. Locking the doors each time he went out was a pain, but he'd seen enough of Kacy-Whoever-She-Was to know that he couldn't trust her not to make a break for it. Hell, if he was in her place, he'd probably do the same thing. No, there was no *probably* to it. He had to give her credit. She had spirit. No, he corrected himself again as he shoved the gate aside and opened the door, *bullheaded* was a more apt description.

The sight that greeted him made him pull up short. Kacy stood before the fireplace. Obviously she had heard him unlocking the door, and faced him now with that Don't-Tread-On-Me look he'd come to admire. Then she turned away and continued to brush her hair dry.

Maybe she could dismiss him that easily, but the same couldn't be said for him. Firelight danced around her, flickering here and there, drawing his attention to the way the long johns fit her slender form. They were Leanne's favorites, the ones with the little yellow flowers, and he'd seen her in them dozens of times over the years. Kacy couldn't be more than two or three inches taller, but the added height stretched the garment enough to make it hug her in all the right places. Kacy was also more curvaceous than his model-thin sister-in-law. He remembered how he and Ray used to tease Leanne about how sexy she was in the long johns, especially when she was pregnant, which had been every other year for the past seven years. Laughing, Leanne would whirl and preen and flirt with Ray until Dan would take his cue and go fishing.

But Kacy wearing them now was no joking matter.

He didn't trust his voice not to betray him, so he said nothing. He stepped through the threshold, discarded the wood, then returned to lock the door.

Kacy still had her back to him and he couldn't stop his gaze from traveling from the top of her head and down the length of her. Had he noticed before her rich dark hair, how the light danced over it, changing the color from deepest brown to auburn and a shade of black he couldn't describe if he'd had to? Or how regally she held her slender shoulders? Or the way her tiny waist curved gracefully into generous hips . . . ?

Damn it to hell! he swore silently, stripping away his hat and coat and hanging them on the pegs by the door. What was the matter with him? Just because the danger had passed was no reason to let his hormones override good sense. He still had things to take care of. And taking a shower was at the top of the list. He stalked to the bathroom and closed the door.

He wasted no time shucking his muddy clothes. His jeans hit the floor and he heard the keys jingle. Taking them out, along with his wallet, he dropped them both into one of his boots, then stepped into the shower.

God, but the hot water spraying across his tense muscles felt good. He scrubbed away the chill and swamp water and mud, then took a cue from his guest and rinsed out his clothes. Hanging there beside hers, his things reminded him of how big and threatening he must appear to her. She had no idea that he wasn't exactly what he appeared to be — a bandit and a kidnapper. She had to be scared out of her wits. If he didn't want her to be more trouble than she already was, he'd have to take special pains to put her fears at rest. The best way to do that, he decided, picking up the scissors and whacking away at the beard, was to keep his distance.

A sudden recollection of her soft brown eyes, filled first with fear, then determination, and finally anger, and her dark hair spilling over her shoulders caused an uncomfortable feeling deep in his solar plexus. Scraping the razor along his jaw, he swore again. Man, he'd really screwed things up and there wasn't a damned thing he could do about it now. What was done was done. Period.

Slapping a handful of aftershave on his freshly shaved face, he studied himself in the mirror. Or was it *his* fears he had to deal with first?

Again he swore. But this time for another reason. He'd forgotten his dry clothes, but unlike Kacy, who had been threatened with being tied up and stuffed in a corner, he had no excuse for leaving his clothes in the other room. Granted, he had been none too happy with his train of thought at the time, but the only reason he could come up with for his carelessness was that he was used to having the place to himself. The only times he ever had to worry about modesty had been when Leanne accompanied him and Ray on their trips to the cabin. Even then, and mostly early on in Leanne's and Ray's marriage, an occasional glimpse of one by the other had caused only minor discomfort. In time they had become like brother and sister, and if one accidentally walked in on the other while dressing, it was no big deal.

But this wasn't Leanne. And his earlier reaction to Kacy was another complication he wasn't prepared to handle.

He opened the door and called her name. When she didn't answer, he secured the towel around his waist and took one tentative step out.

The room was dark, except for the fire, and when he saw her, he felt his lips turn up at the corners. Sitting in the recliner, her long legs curled under her, she had fallen asleep.

Careful not to disturb her, Dan eased to the nearest trunk and found a dry set of clothes. After stepping into his briefs, he pulled on clean, dry jeans and discarded the towel. His gaze kept returning to the sleeping woman. Her head had lolled to one side at an odd angle he knew would make her neck stiff and sore.

Quietly tossing the cushions from the sofa, he pulled out the hide-a-bed and folded back the covers.

On bare feet he padded back to where Kacy slept. His gaze followed the gentle curve of her ear where she'd tucked her hair behind it, went on to regard the delicate angle of her jaw, her flawless skin that made him ache to touch her cheek. It was hard to ignore the pulse at the base of her throat where the long johns were unbuttoned, or the faint rise and fall of her full, firm breasts. So he didn't.

Soundlessly he stood watching her for several long seconds, trying to define the sense of longing that had washed over him when he saw something else. The glint of firelight glancing off metal. Held loosely in her slender fingers he saw a butcher knife, one from his kitchen. A smile crept across his face. She'd found something for protection and was too exhausted to use it. He wanted to wake her and tell her again that he meant her no harm, but he didn't have the heart. She looked so fragile and defenseless in sleep that all he could do was scoop her into his arms and carry her to his bed.

He was glad that she didn't rouse, for if she had, she'd have drawn away instead of winding her arms around his neck and snuggling closer. Her hair, that glorious mane of brown-black curls, brushed against his bare shoulder. Her breath fanned his chest. She smelled of Ivory soap and woman, and a groan caught in his throat.

Suddenly he was consumed with regret and uncertainty and longing. The emotions warred inside him, causing him untold confusion.

It had been a long time since he'd thought of anything except revenge for Ray's death. The idea that a stranger — a beautiful, strong-willed stranger — could elicit such an array of feelings from him when he'd felt dead inside for so long, disarmed him.

Gently, reluctantly, he lowered her to

his bed, covered her with his blanket. He disengaged the knife from her hand and carefully placed it where she would be sure to find it on the trunk beside her.

He should have walked away. Instead he knelt beside her and brushed aside a wisp of dark hair from her forehead. For a fleeting moment the emptiness inside him ebbed, and he ached for the comfort he knew he would find in her arms.

Fighting the urge to crawl in beside her, he stood, then turned on his heel and walked straight to the bar. What the hell was the matter with him? With an angry tug, he uncorked the Wild Turkey, then upended the bottle. The amber liquid burned on its way down, and, to put out the fiery sensation, he pulled another long swig.

Glancing again at Kacy, he threaded his fingers through his still-damp hair. Never had the bed looked so inviting, and, God, he was tired. He drew a weary breath, then swore to himself. He knew before he gathered the discarded sofa cushions that he was going to be the gentleman bandit. She could have the damned bed, he groused, pulling his sleeping bag out from behind the sofa and spreading it out on the cushions he managed to kick into a row in front of the fire.

He grabbed the bottle of Turkey and chugged down several long swallows. He didn't want to think about the woman in his bed or how she'd fouled up all his well-thought-out plans. The alcohol began to take effect and his thoughts fuzzed inside his brain. He didn't want to think about how she would feel lying next to him.

All he wanted was a good night's rest, he told himself. This time the whiskey didn't burn at all going down, and he didn't bother putting the cork back in the bottle. If he drank himself into oblivion again, he wouldn't have to think about how she'd complicated things for him.

5

Kacy sat bolt upright at the loud scraping noise that woke her. It was still dark and raining outside. Her vision wouldn't adjust to the darkness, but she knew instantly that she was in an unfamiliar bed.

'Go back to sleep, Kacy,' a gruff voice said from somewhere in the room.

She clutched the blanket to her breast and willed herself not to scream. With sudden clarity, it all came back: the bank; the long ride from Houston, first in the jalopy, then from the refinery in the pickup; the canoe; the river — the man who had taken her against her will.

'It's jus' the storm blowin' limbs 'cross the roof.' His voice, though husky with sleep, held another quality that immediately heightened her wariness.

Finally her vision cleared. The fire no

longer leapt about with wild and furious heat. Glowing coals now softly bathed the room in an even, comfortable warmth, casting just enough light for Kacy to make out the form on the floor between her and the fireplace. She also saw the empty Wild Turkey bottle lying on its side.

He shifted on his pallet, mumbled something unintelligible, and Kacy fell back on her pillow. He'd been drinking. No good could come from that, she thought, holding her breath and waiting for him to settle back down. When she dared to breathe again, she realized that the bedding held a faint spicy scent that was both pleasing and disturbing. She didn't even remember there being a bed in the room, much less having gotten into it. Her last recollection was of sitting in front of the fireplace, listening to the gentle crackle of the fire and the rain falling outside the window. That, along with the knife she'd scrounged from the kitchen, must have lulled her into a sense of security, allowing her to fall into a deep sleep. She found it hard to believe that he could have opened up the hide-a-bed, then picked her up and put her to bed without waking her. She must have been more tired than she realized.

He was quiet now, and she raised up to make sure he'd gone back to sleep. That's when she saw the butcher knife on the trunk beside her. The word 'confused' took on new meaning. He had found her with the knife and hadn't taken it away when he easily could have. Why? She felt her hackles rise. What was his game? Did he think so little of her ability to defend herself that he got off on letting her have her puny little weapon? She cast an angry glance across the room.

He lay on his back now, the sleeping bag carelessly tossed back to expose a very broad, very muscular, very naked chest. A peculiar sensation started in the pit of Kacy's stomach and began to work its way upward to her throat. She jerked her gaze away from his chest, up to his face. The first thing she noticed was that he'd shaved. The second was that his eyes were open and that he was staring at the ceiling.

Without the beard, his features no longer held their sinister edge. Even more than the day he'd barged into Hawkins's office, she sensed that elusive something about him that made her want to crawl into his soul for a closer look. Remembering the rage and hatred she'd seen then, she tried again to pinpoint what it was about him that touched her. Had it been fear or hurt? Or perhaps sorrow? Kacy felt her heart swell with compassion. Suddenly, and without a shred of doubt, she knew why he'd left her the knife: It was simply his way of telling her that he understood her fear — and that he trusted her.

'Can't sleep, either?'

His voice came out of the blue to startle her. She jumped and looked up to see that he had raised up to rest on one forearm. The smoldering fire at his back cast his face in heavy shadows, but she could feel that he was studying her intently.

'I . . . I was just startled by the storm, that's all.' She hoped she sounded convincing, and burrowed deeper into the covers. It wouldn't do for him to know that she was lying there trying to analyze him. Maybe it was herself she should be trying to understand.

She heard him tossing around, trying to get comfortable, she guessed. Soon the only noises she heard came from outside. The wind howled through the trees while the rain continued to pelt the windows. All in all they were disturbing sounds, sounds that made her thoughts scramble in an attempt to put them out of mind.

'Do you have a name?' She heard her own voice break the silence. She was tired of thinking of him as the sinister *he* or *him* or *the man*. And she'd interpreted his gesture of leaving her the knife as an unspoken truce between them. Truce or not, she still would maintain a certain degree of caution.

For a moment she thought he'd gone back to sleep, or passed out from the half bottle of whiskey he'd consumed. Then he finally answered.

'Jus' call me Dan.' His words slurred slightly. 'Go back to sleep.'

Dan, she thought with relief. Secretly she'd harbored a fear that he'd be a Big Bubba or a Luther or a Buck. Just knowing that he had a common, everyday name gave her peace of mind. And it was a nice name, a strong, masculine name, one that suited him, she thought. She turned over, tried to get comfortable, then found herself on her back again. Sleep seemed bent on eluding her.

'Dan?'

A short stretch of time preceded his weary 'Yeah?'

'Why are there bars on the windows and the door?'

'It's a long story.'

He sounded tired, but the bars had bothered her from the moment she saw them. She knew she wouldn't rest until she knew the answer. And if *she* wasn't going to rest, neither was *he*. She'd try charming the answer out of him.

'Just tell me you're not a card-carrying member of some secret society lobbying to canonize the Marquis de Sade.'

His soft chuckle made her glad of the darkness that hid her smile.

'They wouldn't have me. Said I had too many followers of my own.' The fatigue in his voice overshadowed the humor, and there was a brief pause before he spoke again. 'Until about a year ago, we never bothered to lock up the place. There's always some outdoorsman needing a place to hole up in in bad weather.' He hesitated and Kacy bit back the urge to prod him on. 'But a bunch of teens took advantage of our hospitality one weekend. I appreciate a good party as well as the next guy, but what they didn't destroy they stole.' This time when he stopped talking, she didn't feel the need to encourage him; she waited patiently. 'The idea of holding a beautiful woman prisoner never occurred to me. Feel better?'

'Much.' And she did. She still didn't know what was going on with him, but the feeling that he really wasn't going to hurt her was reinforced. She also wondered who *we* and *us* were, but she wouldn't ask now.

'Dan?'

'Hmmm?'

'Why did you bring me with you?' She had wondered about it before, of course, but now, for some reason, it didn't seem unreasonable to ask about it. 'You must have known how I'd complicate things.'

Limbs clawed at the roof again, giving him time to think before he answered. 'I had no choice.'

'That's no answer.' She heard him take a deep, weary breath and wondered at her reasons for pushing this conversation when he obviously didn't want to talk.

'You could identify me.'

That didn't cut it with her. 'So could

Mr. Hawkins or Miss Ross.' The room grew oppressive with the silence.

'Hawkins could,' he said. 'Miss Ross was too scared to see past the beard.'

Kacy thought about that for a moment. 'So? If Hawkins — '

'Drop it, Kacy.' He sounded irritated. 'If you're not going to sleep, I'll take the bed.'

Kacy recognized the end of a discussion when she heard one. In the quiet that followed she realized something else. She liked the sound of his voice. The resonant timbre made her feel safe from harm.

Dammit, she swore silently, *you're not going to be one of those dim-witted victims who falls head over heels for her captor*. It wasn't an uncommon phenomenon, according to the talk-show experts, especially if the woman was alone or unhappy or in a bad relationship. But Kacy was none of those things.

Why do you have to make me hurt you? Ted's angry words flew at her from nowhere. He had always been quick to fault her whenever he lost his temper. Nothing she ever did had been good enough.

Forgive me, Kacy. Please. I'll never lay a hand on you again. Remorseful and teary-eyed, he would plead with her until she forgave him. But always in the back of her mind lurked the knowledge that love wasn't supposed to hurt, at least not physically.

The memories insisted on invading her mind, memories of the feelings she'd had for Ted — right 'til the day she'd lost their baby . . .

From some inner well of forgotten pain, tears she thought were behind her made their way to her eyes. Roughly she brushed them away and rolled to her side. She didn't want to talk anymore. All she wanted to think about was home and Mandy. Her gaze locked on the knife. Forcing her eyes closed, she left it where it lay — out in the open and close at hand.

Morning broke quietly, its splendor revealed little by little as dawn cleared the stand of pine and cypress trees behind the cabin. Winter's icy breath clung to everything within sight. Crystalline icicles hung from tree limbs and off the eave of the roof while a heavy vapor rose above the flooded river bottom.

Dan revered the scene through a veil of frost that laced the window over the sink. In a few short hours the mystical illusion would be despoiled by the first warming rays of sunshine, or by the rain, whichever prevailed today.

He'd witnessed the spectacle many times over the years, sometimes alone, at others with his brother while they savored their morning coffee. But today there was no brotherly razzing, no shared anticipation of what the day might hold. Today there were only the woodlands and the memories, memories so strong that they filled him with the pain of accepting that his brother was gone. How was it possible to feel this empty and dead inside when there was so much pain, so many different emotions roiling around in his head and his heart?

He'd felt this way only once before in his life, eight years ago when his Ellie left him. From that experience he'd learned that only time would heal the wound. But Ellie's death had been from natural causes. Ray's had been a senseless, ruthless, calculated murder.

Both hands braced against the kitchen counter, Dan went over it all for the hundredth time. How had he been so blind? Looking back, he could almost pinpoint the day Ray had gotten in over his head. All he needed, Dan remembered Ray explaining, was twenty-five thousand dollars for a certificate of deposit as collateral for his small-business loan, and, no, he insisted, he wouldn't let Dan back him. Dan's money would be safe and drawing interest while Ray worked to make Ray-Lea Construction the success Wilder Construction had grown to be. Less than a week later, Ray had started acting funny, talking about sending Leanne and the boys to visit her folks in Colorado so he could concentrate on his work.

Suddenly the pain in Dan's head turned into a full-fledged, pounding headache. His mouth tasted like raw sewage smelled.

Even now the frustration of not being able to get his brother to confide in him ate away at Dan's insides. Then there had been the accident and so many unanswered questions. His grip on the edge of the cabinet tightened. And, like throwing gasoline on a raging fire, Michaelson's presence at the funeral had added to Dan's confusion and anger. All the special agent had been willing to say was that Ray had been a fine man who died trying to do the right thing.

Absently Dan massaged the muscles

of his neck and fought the images which continued to haunt him: Michaelson, somber-faced and guilt-ridden, telling him what a hero Ray had been; the coffin lid closing to shut out Ray's lifeless face; the bittersweet smell of too many flowers. And the tears. God, Leanne's tears had been the hardest to bear simply because there had been none of his own.

But Michaelson made one serious mistake. He mentioned Hawkins's name. That was all Dan needed. A place to start.

A restless noise behind him drew his gaze from the wintry scene outside to Kacy sleeping peacefully in his bed. He smiled. Her feet were uncovered again. For the third time in the past hour, he went to the bed and pulled the blanket over her bare feet. And for the umpteenth time he regretted having to involve an innocent in this nightmare. He swore softly and turned away. What was done was done. He'd have to make the best of the situation — and that included seeing to it that no harm came to her.

★ ★ ★

Hugo Michaelson was usually still trying to pry his eyelids open and saturate his system with caffeine at six A.M. But not this morning. He had a stop to make on his way to the office.

His experienced eye took in every detail of the spic-and-span playroom of Wee Care Day Care. From the freshly painted Disney characters that graced the walls to the multicolored game-board carpet covering the reading area in the center of the room, it was obvious that the owners took great pride in providing both a clean and pleasant environment for their children.

'Detective Michaelson.' Mary Martin, a petite brunette with a trim figure and pert features, greeted him with a smile that did what the one cup of coffee hadn't been able to — made him sit up and take notice. 'Thank you for coming by early.' She motioned for him to take one of the dwarf chairs surrounding the dwarf table around which she was busy placing finger paints and large sheets of paper.

She stopped what she was doing to give him her full attention. 'I'm sorry I couldn't answer your questions yesterday. I was running late with the after-school pickups. That's usually Kacy's job, but . . . ' Her words trailed off, then she pulled her shoulders straighter. 'Shall we get started? Things will get pretty hectic around here in about . . . ' She glanced up at the smiling Mickey Mouse clock on the wall. ' . . . twenty-five minutes.'

Distracted momentarily by the way her artfully arched eyebrows pulled together over whiskey-colored eyes, Michaelson reached into his pocket for his note pad and pen. 'I need to get a few more details from you concerning your friend . . . ' He glanced down at his notes. ' . . . Kacy Angelle.' Looking back at the woman sitting across from him, he forgot how uncomfortable he was with his legs shoved up under his chin.

Mary hesitated, then stood. 'Excuse me,' she said, leaving him and going to the door that led to the hallway he'd followed to get to this room. 'Justine, would you keep Mandy and Andrew and Charlie busy for a few minutes?' Smiling, she closed the door and returned to the activity table. 'I'd rather Kacy's little girl didn't overhear any of this,' she explained, taking her seat across the table from Michaelson. 'All I've told her and my boys is that Kacy's away for a few days.

'About three-thirty yesterday,' she went on, 'Kacy called to ask me to watch Mandy for her. She sounded strange; kind of worried and a lot scared. Like someone was listening to every word she was saying. And, as I mentioned, she hadn't made the after-school pickups.'

'Has she ever done anything like this before?' Michaelson knew the answer, but had to ask it. 'You know, just picked up and left on the spur of the moment for a few days, with a friend?'

Mary's tiny chin jutted out. 'Kacy's not like that. If you knew all she's been through you wouldn't even ask such a question.'

Michaelson put his pen aside. 'It might help me to know what she's been through.' He saw by the determined set of her red-tinted lips that she was intensely loyal to her friend. He waited for her to make up her mind about confiding in him.

'Kacy's been divorced almost eleven years.' She looked toward the closed door again. This time when she spoke, her voice held a frosty bite. 'The bastard beat her one time too many, caused a miscarriage that left her unable to have children. That's the reason she doesn't date much and why Mandy was such a godsend for her.' Mary hesitated. 'Anyway, after the miscarriage, Kacy finally got enough courage to end the marriage and put

119

herself through college, which is where we met.' She met his gaze momentarily. 'I was doing pretty much the same thing, except my ex never laid a hand on me.' A becoming blush spread across her face when she realized she'd digressed. 'About five years ago, she and I started our day-care center.'

Michaelson had heard the expression 'positively glowed with pride,' but until this moment he'd never actually seen it firsthand. He wasn't aware that she'd stopped talking until his eyes met hers. Embarrassed at being caught studying him as closely as he was regarding her, Mary dropped her gaze and blushed an even deeper shade of pink. He fought back the smile that tried to find its way to his lips. That women found him attractive was something he'd gotten used to and he usually enjoyed the chase. This woman was no exception, but somehow it was different with her. He almost swore out loud when he realized what it was. He liked her. Not just as a woman, a conquest, as it were.

But as a person.

'We couldn't believe how good business was, how fast we grew,' she went on, apparently unaware of the unprofessional turn his thoughts had taken. 'Everything was going great until we got that notice from Mr. Hawkins about our loan. That's why Kacy was at the bank in the first place.'

'Loan?' Michaelson sat up straighter. The highly trained professional was back. 'You and Mrs. Angelle have a business loan with Marcus Hawkins?'

Mary nodded. 'Yes. And it's *Miss* Angelle. Since there were no children, Kacy took back her maiden name after the divorce.'

He glanced across the table to see the woman he was already thinking of as Mary instead of Mrs. Martin staring at the hands in her lap.

'I can't help blaming that hothead who stormed in to take her appointment that day. If it hadn't been for him, she wouldn't have been at the bank yesterday.'

Michaelson leaned forward, instinct telling him that he was on to something important. 'What hothead? What day?'

Mary must have sensed that his interest had been piqued, because she raised her gaze to meet his. 'Three weeks ago, the very day we received the notice about our loan, Kacy went in to see Mr. Hawkins. Before she could see him, this guy came barreling in and roughed up Hawkins pretty good.' She paused, waiting for Michaelson to look up from his notes. 'This is important, isn't it?' She eyed him squarely.

'I'm not sure.' He wasn't a man to lie. 'Anything else?'

Mary looked as though she was trying to recall every detail she'd been told. 'The only other thing she told me was that the man who caused such a scene looked like he'd been hurt real bad. You know, she saw it in his eyes when he spoke to her.'

'He talked to her?' Maybe there was a tie-in after all, Michaelson thought.

'Yes. He told her to take her business

someplace else. I remember Kacy saying it sounded like he was warning her about something.'

Michaelson tried not to let his thoughts show. 'What about Hawkins?' Changing subjects seemed like a good idea.

'Kacy said he was so shook up that he canceled the rest of his appointments. That's why she was there yesterday. It was his first day back from a three-week vacation. She wanted to get our problem settled before the deadline.' Her voice grew more shaky with each word until finally she said, 'Violence of any kind really rattles Kacy. I'm afraid of what she'll do if he tries to . . . to hurt her . . . ' She had to stop.

Michaelson lost the quick wrestling match between professional ethics and his need to put her mind at ease. 'If it's who I think it is, he won't.'

'What aren't you telling me?' Mary wasn't a patient person, Michaelson soon found out.

'Anything I could tell you at this point would be nothing but speculation.' He hoped his official FBI tone would dissuade her from further probing.

'You know, if I hadn't gone to Taylor's Garage to pick up Kacy's van, I wouldn't have known anything about this. Mr. Taylor was the one who told me about all the cops at the bank. I haven't heard a word about it on the news.' Again her eyebrows pulled together. She was sharp.

'We'll be releasing information later this morning, Mrs. Martin.' Maybe that would pacify her.

Mary eyed him with a look that said *Okay, I won't push.* 'It's *Ms.* Martin, Detective.'

The detective returned her smile. 'Can you tell me one other thing, Ms. Martin?' he asked, getting back to business.

'I'll try.'

'Was Southside Savings and Loan the name that appeared on your loan papers?'

'I'm not sure, but now that you

mention it, I don't think it was.' Her forehead wrinkled in thought. 'With all the savings and loan problems over the years, we didn't think anything about the names being different.' She cocked her head to one side. 'I don't see what our loan has to do any of this.'

Michaelson had his hunches, but for the time being he'd keep them to himself. If the man who took Miss Angelle was who he thought he was, she wasn't in any real danger, at least not from him. But *why* had he taken her?

'Would you happen to have those loan papers — '

Mary stopped him by shaking her head. 'No, Kacy had them with her. She said she wasn't leaving the bank until Hawkins explained how they could threaten to take over Wee Care if we didn't come up with the entire loan balance by the middle of December.'

A rush of relief and anger washed over Michaelson at the same time. *That* was the connection. Now if only he could figure out what Wilder was up to.

6

The air was fresh though chilly, but Kacy felt as if she was suffocating. Lying on her side, she searched for the edge of the bed with one foot, then flipped the blanket back to leave her calves and feet uncovered — again. Much better, she thought with a groggy sigh, then tucked the blanket snugly under her chin. Ever since she could remember, she couldn't rest unless her feet were out in the open.

No sooner had she settled back into a light slumber than the aroma of freshly perked coffee and frying bacon tugged her back to semiconsciousness. She sniffed the air, the smells reminding her of childhood mornings at home, of her mother welcoming Kacy and her four younger sisters into a cozy kitchen before sending them on their way to school. So pleasant were the thoughts that she smiled and snuggled deeper into the covers. Those had been the good times, before Poppa died, before Momma remarried. Life after that became a living hell.

Even in sleep, Kacy felt the joy leave her heart. She hadn't fully understood the reasons, but remembered rationalizing at the time that with five hungry children to feed, Momma had little choice but to endure a bad situation. Bent on escaping the nightmare of an alcoholic stepfather, Kacy had failed to see the warning signs that should have stopped her from marrying Ted. But being the oldest, she let her dreams of providing a refuge for her sisters blind her to his propensity toward violence. Her one-year marriage turned out to be the biggest tragedy of all . . .

She wasn't aware of the knot slowly tightening in her solar plexus until her eyes opened. A light glowed from somewhere, and, momentarily disoriented from her drowsy journey into the past, she glanced toward it. At first, she didn't recognize the man standing with his back to her. She tried to clear her thoughts, to remember where she was and how she'd gotten there. He took a step sideways, giving her a glimpse of his profile.

Suddenly, and with startling clarity, it all came back. This was the man who had dragged her through hell and high water and away from Mandy.

She closed her eyes in an effort to block out the guilt she felt for having slept so soundly through the night. How could she have done that when Mandy had probably cried herself to sleep in Mary's arms? Kacy's heart felt like it was going to explode. Did her baby feel deserted, alone, and frightened? No, she thought, forcing herself to calm down. Mandy wasn't alone. She had Mary and her sons. And she would have remembered to take Radar with her. The cuddly teddy bear was her favorite stuffed animal, the one Kacy had given her on their first Christmas together.

Feeling stronger now, and careful not to make a sound, she sat up. He seemed to sense her gaze on him and looked her way.

'Coffee?' He held up an aluminum percolator and she gave him a grateful nod. 'Light and sweet, I'll bet,' he said with a grimace that eased her tension.

Again she nodded, noting with a mixture of disbelief and relief that the knife still lay on the trunk beside her. Tugging at the legs of the long johns that had ridden up during the night, she approached the cup he placed on the bar between them. She didn't miss the way his eyes flicked over the length of her, but she ignored it by glancing around the kitchen.

The small area was far from modern, although she guessed that as river camps went, this one would probably rate an A-plus for being clean and well kept. Most likely she wouldn't have noticed the butane smell that lingered in the air if her own stove hadn't been electric, or that the refrigerator looked to be better than twenty years old if she hadn't been forced to buy a new one just last week when her own had quit working. The aqua Formica dated the simple structure — almost to the year — and although it was chipped in places along the edges, it was still passable. A box of powdered milk sat beside a plate overflowing with crisply fried bacon; a fine dusting of flour covered the counter top to his immediate left.

'Be a few minutes.' He added flour to the bacon drippings covering the bottom of the cast-iron skillet, then seasoned it with salt and pepper. He stirred the browning mixture with the confidence of a man accustomed to doing for himself. 'Might as well freshen up while I make the gravy.' Fishing a dishcloth from the sink filled with sudsy water, he wrung it out, then wiped both the counter and stovetops clean.

Another aroma mingled with the scent of bacon and coffee, and Kacy's mouth began to water. 'Biscuits?'

Dan glanced over his shoulder. 'From scratch.' A smile that radiated everything from warmth to mischief dazzled her from the short distance that separated them.

The man's amazing, she thought, trudging off to her morning toilet. From the amount of alcohol she knew he'd put away during the night, he shouldn't be able to hold his head up, much less go about daily chores with a smile like that.

The space heater in the bathroom was doing its job. The room greeted her with a gentle wave of toasty warmth. She splashed water on her face, then groaned at the sight staring back at her. Her hair was a tousled mass of dark-brown curls, her eyes puffy from sleep. She would have killed for a toothbrush. But it was the reflection of the empty shower curtain rod in the mirror that made her forehead wrinkle.

'Where're my clothes?' she called, opening the door just enough that she could see him pouring thick white gravy into an earthenware bowl.

'They were still wet, so I hung them on the mantelpiece.' He placed the gravy bowl on the bar. 'Couldn't find your shoes,' he added absently.

'They came off in the mud when we got out of the truck last night.'

His dark eyebrows pulled together. She couldn't help noticing that the emerald of his eyes perfectly matched the green in the plaid flannel shirt he now sported.

'Remind me to find you a pair of socks,' he told her, opening the oven door, then closing it again. 'It'll be a while before the biscuits are done. Take your coffee and warm yourself by the fire.'

He dismissed her by turning back to the sink to wash the skillet so she retreated to the adjoining room, realizing as she stood before the fire what a cozy scene they were acting out. To an outsider looking in, it might appear that they were an average couple, enjoying a

132

quiet moment before their morning meal.

The thought was abruptly chopped off by the sight of her lacy bra and panties hanging between her clothes and his. He couldn't have placed them more strategically if he'd purposely planned to embarrass her. She gave Dan a wary glance. He was too busy checking the biscuits again to notice her discreetly take the wisps of black and stuff them into the pocket of her still-damp jacket.

That's when she realized for the first time how flimsy the long johns were. Tiny yellow rosettes dotted the white thermal fabric, fabric that was functional enough, though it left much to be desired in the modesty department. Suddenly she was acutely aware of every feminine curve — and of the fact that her underwear was hiding out in the pocket of her jacket.

'It's ready when you are.'

Kacy suppressed the urge to fold her arms across her chest as she joined him at the breakfast bar. She hadn't eaten a bite since lunch yesterday, and her modesty was soon forgotten as she bit into the best-tasting biscuits and cream gravy she'd ever eaten.

They ate in silence, neither seeming to have anything to say to the other. As Kacy sipped her coffee, she noticed the contents of his wallet spread out to dry on one end of the bar: his driver's license, several credit cards, and what she suspected were hunting and fishing licenses.

Curiosity got the better of her, and, lowering her lashes, she read the name on his driver's license, *Daniel Q. Wilder*, and his address, which told her absolutely nothing since she didn't recognize the street. Quickly she scanned the other information. *Color Eyes: Green*, which she already knew; *Height: 6'0"*; and after some quick mental calculations, she learned from his birth date that he'd turned thirty-seven last month. The likeness of him on the right side of the plastic document smiled back at her with careless charm. In the time they had been together, he had graced her with a smile or two, but they had been more to reassure her than anything else. This one was full of life and she couldn't help wondering if the officer who had taken the photo had been a woman.

'Is Kacy short for something?'

She jerked her gaze up to see him studying her intently. 'What?'

He leaned back to grab the coffeepot from the stove behind him. 'Kacy,' he said, warming both their cups with fresh coffee. 'It's an unusual name for a woman. I just wondered if it was a nickname.' Clearly the silence was wearing thin on him and the way he said her name, the softening of his voice, was a welcome intrusion.

'No, it's just plain Kacy. Nothing special.'

The tension between them waned, leaving Kacy with the absurd notion that under different circumstances they might have been friends. From the glimmer in his eyes, she suspected his thoughts had taken a similar turn.

Silence fell upon them again as they sipped from their mugs. The way his gaze seemed to take in every detail of her face unnerved her, bringing back the disturbing truth: They weren't friends, nor even acquaintances. He was the man who held her fate in his hands.

'Just-Plain-Kacy-Nothing-Special what?' He graced her with a smile she intuitively knew had stopped many a heart in mid-flutter over the years.

Regardless of who he was, it had the same effect on her now and that startled her. *This is crazy*, she chided herself. She wasn't a starry-eyed teenager any more than she was socially involved with Daniel Q. Wilder. She also wasn't in any mood to be humored or patronized or charmed or whatever else he had in mind. 'Look, I don't know what — '

'Relax.' He stood abruptly, silencing her in the process. 'Just thought it would ease the tension to talk. I was wrong.' Oddly enough, the icy edge she heard in his voice left her with an unexpected pang of regret.

'The dishes are all yours.' Without so much as a glance at her, he collected his personal belongings and carelessly stuffed them back inside his wallet. He was gone before she could protest, back to the den, where he proceeded to roll up his bed roll.

The woman of the nineties in her didn't take kindly to being ordered to clean up. The captive, however, was still too unsure of her captor's temperament not to do as she was told. Besides, she noted with a small degree of satisfaction, so far he'd treated her fairly. In fact, he'd done all the work. As she watched, he shoved his sleeping bag behind the sofa, then straightened the bedding on her bed. In one fluid motion the hide-a-bed disappeared into the sofa. And since he'd cooked, it wouldn't kill her to wash a few dishes, she knew.

He was one of those people who

cleaned as he went, so the only dishes left were their plates, flatware, and coffee mugs. The chore took only a few minutes, and she wiped at the fog covering the window as she waited for the sink to drain. Her hand flew to her lips to stifle her horrified gasp.

Last night had been so stormy that she couldn't see two feet in front of her, much less what lay ahead. Now that she could, she wasn't sure she felt any better.

The cabin sat perched upon a slightly sloping knoll encompassed on three sides by woods. The fourth side, the front, she remembered, faced the river. Enough morning sun filtered through the dense stand of trees for her to see that all the surrounding land was under water, leaving the cabin literally stranded in the middle of a small island. The splendor of the misty veil created by morning fog and sunlight was lost on Kacy. All she saw was a domain that was as alien to her as another galaxy would be. He hadn't been bluffing last night — there was no way out by land.

'Beautiful, isn't it?'

Kacy didn't hear him approach and jumped back, colliding with the solid wall of his body. Every muscle in her body tensed. She did her best to shrivel up, to make herself smaller when he leaned forward, pinning her between his arms and the counter. Why couldn't she remember how to breathe?

It took two tries for her to form a coherent thought. 'I . . . I can't believe it.'

His sleeves were rolled up a fold or two, leaving his forearms bare. She swallowed and stared at the strong, thick wrists, the long fingers wrapped around the edge of the sink. His breath stirred the hair next to her ear and a heavy sensation settled in her chest. She stiffened and gathered what she still possessed of her composure.

'Please, you're scaring me.' Her voice came out in a whisper that she immediately wanted to swallow. He didn't move closer, as she feared he might, nor did he back away.

A moment passed before he softly said, 'I know.' His voice was low and husky. Its timbre sent shock waves of warning through her. 'You're just very tempting in those long johns.' The last thing she expected was for him to back off, but he did, leaving Kacy to grasp the counter for support when her knees almost gave away. She hung her head in relief and saw a chambray shirt and a pair of neatly rolled socks lying on the counter where his hands had been.

She looked up to see his reflection in the window glass disappearing and marveled at the myriad emotions roiling around inside her. She felt weak and confused, frightened and alone, things she had forced out of her life little by little over the years. At the same time she was amazed by the strength she'd shown by not falling apart every time he came near her. And, oddly, she also felt more alive than she had felt in a long, long while.

Stunned by the thought, she turned around to see him settled at the bar with the athletic bag in front of him and a small box to one side. Music she hadn't noticed before, a popular country tune, filled the room while Dan took the paper bag that contained the Tex-Oil parking permits and the McDonald's remnants out and tossed them into the fireplace.

The pile of wet trail markers at the far end of the bar went unnoticed because her attention was focused on the tightly banded stacks of twenty- and hundred-dollar bills lying in front of him. Although it appeared to be a lot of money, it hardly seemed worth the risks he'd taken. That's when she saw two computer disks beside the box.

He inclined his head, indicating the shirt and socks in her hand. 'Go ahead and put those on.'

Distracted by the money and her thoughts, she slipped on the shirt, then sat down across from him. Until he mentioned the socks, she hadn't realized her feet were cold. The white athletic socks were much too large, but she relished the warmth they provided.

' . . . and an unexpected development in yesterday's holdup of a Houston bank,' the disc jockey's voice broke into the silence that had fallen. 'This and other news after these messages.'

Dan swiveled on his bar stool, stood, and started toward the sound system ensconced in the bookshelves. He turned up the volume on the radio, then calmly returned to the kitchen.

Anxious, Kacy waited through two commercials, one for a tire dealership boasting of matching prices on name-brand tires, and one for a pharmacy promising to honor all competitors' coupons. Finally the DJ came back on the air.

'Authorities are speculating on the reason a lone bandit took the owner of Wee Care Day Care hostage in yesterday's robbery of Southside Savings and Loan. Thirty-year-old Kacy

Angelle has been missing since approximately one o'clock yesterday afternoon, the same time the robber was making his escape with over one hundred thousand dollars.'

Kacy's gaze flew to the stacks of money. She had no way of knowing for certain, but at a glance she'd bet there wasn't more than twenty thousand dollars, thirty, tops, on that bar.

'Described as a white male in his mid-to-late thirties, the suspect is approximately six feet tall, one hundred and seventy pounds. He has shaggy black hair, and at the time of the holdup, he was wearing a beard. Miss Angelle stands five nine, is of slender build, and her eyes and hair are brown.' A brief description of both their clothes followed. 'The man is armed and considered dangerous. And now for the weather. Clear and cold for most of the day, but look for more rain later in the evening . . . '

Kacy leaned forward and plucked the bag off the bar. There was nothing else inside. 'Where's the rest of the money?' She couldn't believe she was being so bold.

Dan closed the small cardboard box that now contained the money. 'Don't believe everything you hear on the news.' Calmly taking the bag from her, he placed the box inside it, then slipped the computer disks into his shirt pocket. When he stood to tower over her, Kacy stubbornly refused to get out of his way.

'There's nowhere near a hundred thousand dollars in that bag,' she persisted. 'What's going on?'

He sidestepped her with without answering. 'What size shoe do you wear?' he asked instead, taking his coat and slipping it on.

'What?' Now she couldn't believe what he was saying.

'Shoes,' he repeated, ignoring her. 'What size do you wear?'

Kacy brought both arms up in a gesture of frustration. 'I don't believe this. I'm standing here talking with a crazy man.' Forgetting her state of dress, she stalked toward him. His eyes quickly reminded her that she was braless. 'Eight and a half,' she sputtered, embarrassed.

'Anything else you need?'

Kacy's eyes widened in comprehension. 'You're leaving me here alone?' The thought was terrifying. He couldn't be serious.

He settled his hat on his head as if nothing were amiss. 'I have things to take care of — '

'I won't be any trouble,' she promised, meaning every word. 'I can be dressed in two minutes. Just don't leave me alone.' She scampered for her clothes.

'Stop,' he ordered, his tone harsher than she'd ever heard it, his grasp tight and unrelenting on her arm.

Instinct took over and with a ferocity that surprised them both, she yanked free. 'Don't *ever* touch me like that again.' She heard the tremor in her own voice, saw the muscles along his jawline

145

tense. For a moment she feared she'd gone too far, then his features softened.

'I can't take you with me, Kacy.' The tenderness in his voice matched the compassion in his eyes. 'There's plenty of wood in the bin, and more on the porch. And there's enough food in the pantry and ice box to hold you over for days in case I don't make it back tonight.'

Kacy felt the trembling start in her middle and work its way outward. He was actually leaving her alone in this godforsaken wilderness.

'You can go outside, but stay close to the cabin. I wasn't exaggerating about the alligators and snakes,' she heard him saying through the roaring in her ears. 'And in case you get any bright ideas about going for help, my closest neighbors are more than three miles away. *Upriver*,' he stressed. 'And on the Texas side.' He said each word clearly, distinctly while he held her gaze with his own. 'Now, is there anything else you need?'

Kacy knew it was useless to argue. Her shoulders slumped in defeat. 'I need to be home with Mandy.' Her answer was barely a whisper until she looked up at him and said stiffly, 'But I'll settle for a toothbrush.'

* * *

Dan reached the pickup less than an hour later. Going with the current downriver was much faster and easier than the trip the previous night. Normally it was a trip Dan enjoyed, but the farther he got from the cabin, the worse he felt. Good reason or no, he was guilty of keeping a mother from her daughter.

He yanked the door open with a vengeance and flung the bag inside. *Damn it*, he swore, hating the weakness that threatened his objective. There was another mother and three small boys with no one to depend on now except him. Blood was thicker than water. Slamming the door closed, he swore again. The sooner he got the disks in the mail and the money in an account for Leanne, the sooner this mess would be over. Then he could see to it that Kacy got back to her little girl.

The water had risen another couple of inches, he noted, dragging the canoe to the back of the truck. He couldn't take a chance on not being able to get this far when he returned. He'd have to relocate the canoe. Dropping the tailgate, he hoisted one end of the boat into the cargo bed, then angled it all the way in. Quickly tying it down, he fished the keys out of his pocket, then sloshed his way to the cab. It would mean paddling a longer distance, but he didn't have much choice. Even if it didn't rain another drop, he'd have to leave the truck on higher ground tonight.

He unzipped the bag and pulled out a handful of trail markers. Finding his way out was easy enough by daylight, but without the markers he'd never find his way back to the canoe after dark.

The key slid into the ignition as it always did, but nothing happened when he turned it. Not a sound. Dan sat there, disbelieving, then tried again with the same result.

The expletive that erupted from him was as colorful as it was imaginative. Something like this would be expected from the clunker he'd ditched yesterday, but the truck was brand new. Swearing again, he raised the hood with the hope that this wasn't an omen of how the rest of the day would go.

7

'Hello!' Kacy called from the front porch, more loudly this time. The sun was sinking into the treetops to the west as dusk made its claim on the day. 'Can anyone hear me?' She listened intently, hoping, praying that someone would answer. All she heard was the sound of water rushing past the cabin and through the surrounding underbrush. Maybe her imagination was playing tricks on her, she thought as she leaned against one of the natural log posts that held up the porch. Maybe it hadn't been a gunshot she'd heard.

Although she'd felt free to roam at will, scattered showers and the brisk December wind had kept her indoors most of the day. Only when her supply of wood inside dwindled to nothing did she venture out as far as the top step. Her only companion, the radio, had kept her posted on the latest storm front moving along the upper Gulf Coast of Southeast Texas. Compared to the past few weeks, today with its sunshine and warmer temperature had been a boon to her fragile state of mind.

Drawing her jacket tighter over her sweater, she glanced up at the storm-dark sky. The weather wouldn't hold much longer. And the concern she felt became suddenly alarming when she couldn't decide if she was more afraid of being stranded out here alone or that Dan might not be all right.

The thought spawned questions she was unable or unwilling to answer. To put the issue straight in her own mind, she staunchly told herself that since he was the only one who knew her whereabouts, her interest in his welfare was nothing more than a matter of self-preservation.

Loath to see the light of day waning, she lingered there a moment longer. Never had she been in such a desolate place. The forest was coming to life with evening sounds, noises that to her city ears were at once eerie and ethereal. The chattering of several small animals, squirrels she guessed, drew her attention to the thick stand of trees off to her right, but the motion of the limbs in the breeze made it impossible to see the tiny creatures. Then, as if on cue, the wind blustered across the Sabine, carrying with it a howl much like the one she'd heard last night. The combination sent a shiver coursing through her. The chill reminded her of her chore, and clumsily she stacked as much wood as she could carry across one arm, then headed back inside for what she hoped was the last time.

It had taken her six trips, but at last the wood bin was filled to capacity. Immensely satisfied with her accomplishment, Kacy tossed two more logs on the fire before curling up in the recliner to wait for the room to lose its bite.

Quite possibly this had been the longest day in her life. She'd spent the better part of it rummaging through Dan's belongings without knowing what she was looking for. The only incriminating things she turned up were another bottle of bourbon, unopened, and a ballpoint pen with a voluptuous redhead in the barrel whose bikini disappeared little by little when it was held in the writing position.

In the end, she'd wound up trying to gain entry to the gun cabinet again. The unsuccessful attempt left her more frustrated than anything else, and soon she found herself so bored that she resorted to trying to figure out just exactly how the disappearing bikini worked. That held her attention for all of thirty seconds.

Her antidote for boredom or worry had always been activity, so she decided to straighten up a bit. She swept, fluffed a couple of pillows, positioned the recliner closer to the fire, cleaned out the silverware drawer — all of which took no more than thirty minutes. Next she browsed the hearth-to-ceiling bookshelves that flanked each side of the fireplace. Books ranging from fiction and nonfiction to biographies and the arts and sciences were nestled haphazardly among magazines and record albums and audio tapes. The latest best-selling thriller by her favorite author caught her eye and she settled in for however much time she would have to read. Big mistake, she realized midway through seven chapters. All she'd managed to do was to scare herself silly.

Since her only source of information about the outside world came from the radio, she opted for listening to it rather than choosing from the wide selection of music she found neatly organized on the shelves. The only stations she could tune in inundated her with country music. Not that she didn't like country music — to the contrary, she enjoyed it on occasion. But even a bred-and-born Texan could appreciate only so many songs lamenting cheating lovers, beer-chugging buddies, or long, lonesome nights.

Whenever Mandy entered her thoughts, which was often early in the day, the memories served only to bring her more distress than comfort. The idea that she might never see her daughter again was like a dagger through her heart. Her only solace came in the knowledge that Mandy was safe with Mary. The important thing for Kacy to do at this point, she convinced herself, was to concentrate on surviving this ordeal.

Suddenly chilled, she stood and briskly rubbed both her arms. Back and forth she paced before the fire, fretting and fuming, first about being alone, then about whether or not Dan was safe. Remembering the ease with which he'd maneuvered the canoe through the turbulent weather last night did little to alleviate her worry. No matter how confident she was that he was more than fit to make the journey, she couldn't help thinking about the things that could happen to him out there alone.

Stop it, she commanded herself, pulling up short between the chair and the fireplace. *He's okay and you'll be okay.* The mantelpiece was right at her eye level and a framed photo captured her attention. She didn't know why she hadn't noticed it before. Taking it down, she studied the likeness of Dan and another man standing on the front steps of this very cabin. Sunlight glistened off Dan's dark, hatless head. The twinkle in his eyes and the smile on his lips put her in mind of a mischievous youth who had just been caught in some misdeed, but who also knew that he could talk his way out of any punishment. She'd glimpsed this side of his nature once or twice, a side she was surprised to realize she was curious to know better.

Uncomfortable with the thought, she focused her attention on the other man. Not quite as tall as Dan, nor as solidly built, the man was younger, probably by a good five years. One arm was thrown carelessly around Dan's shoulder, and he, too, was smiling as though they had just pulled off the prank to end all pranks.

Outside, rain started falling again — not just a drizzle as it had done off and on all day, but a downpour that blocked out everything else. Trying to ignore it, Kacy sat down and tucked her feet under her. She glanced down at the photo again, this time letting her thumb caress the miniature of Dan's rugged features.

Funny, she thought, she didn't think of him like this, smiling and carefree, content with the world. During her captivity, he'd graced her with a smile or two, and she'd even seen his tender side. How many fugitives would stop in the middle of a getaway to let his hostage make arrangements for the care of her child? Or leave her a weapon as a token gesture of trust?

Intuitively Kacy knew there was more

to Dan's story than she knew. But what? The room was warm now, friendly, and she rested her head against the chair back and closed her eyes. Images raced around inside her head like a movie in fast-forward mode. She saw everything as clearly as it had been that day three weeks ago in the reception area outside Hawkins's office. Even then, Dan's brooding demeanor had intrigued her. And what was it he had said to her on his way out? *Do yourself a favor. Take your business elsewhere.* She remembered thinking at the time that he was warning her against something, but what could it have been when they didn't even know each other?

The scene continued to replay itself in her mind's eye. Details she hadn't thought important at the time came tumbling back. Hawkins hadn't wanted Security called in. Why? And Miss Ross had told her that Wee Care's loan information wasn't in the computer, that Hawkins didn't like others snooping into his 'Special Accounts.' Her weary mind was a jumble of thoughts that raced around and over each other in a frustrating and confusing game of Twenty Questions.

She yawned and reclined the chair, hardly able to keep her eyes open, but intent on mulling it all out. And just this morning the news bulletin had reported that one hundred thousand dollars had been taken in the robbery. Kacy knew firsthand that that wasn't the case. She'd been with Dan from the moment he stepped foot out of the bank, and there couldn't possibly have been that amount of money in that bag. Why the discrepancy?

Rain continued its melodious tattoo on the roof, and Kacy's eyelids grew heavier. Things weren't adding up. Another yawn and she felt sleep overtaking her. The fire, the rain, the day's inactivity all worked together to leave her lethargic and more than a little muddle-brained. That had to account for her being unable to piece it all together. For the moment, she thought, hugging the photo to her breast, it was enough that she was warm and dry.

As she dropped off, she felt secure in the knowledge that a man who wanted to know her shoe size couldn't possibly intend to harm her.

* * *

Dan entered the cabin cautiously. The first thing he'd noticed from the landing was that there were no lights on inside. Exactly what that meant, he wasn't sure, but he wasn't taking any chances. He'd done everything humanly possible to convince Kacy that he meant her no harm, but with the entire day to herself, he wouldn't be surprised if her imagination hadn't spurred her into rash action. A scared woman with an eight-inch butcher knife would be a handful for any man, so he prepared himself for whatever she might have in store for him.

He hadn't allowed for engine trouble. Consequently his trip back to Houston and his errands had taken longer than he anticipated. It had been dark well over an hour and his eyes were already accustomed to the moonless night, so the faint light cast by the crackling fire was more than enough for him to see. Every taut muscle in his body relaxed when he saw Kacy nestled peacefully in the recliner. He also saw the photograph clutched to her breast. The knife was nowhere to be seen.

Careful not to disturb her, he returned to the porch to retrieve the bags he'd abandoned just moments earlier, then placed them on the bar. As he stripped away his soggy hat and coat and hung them by the door, he noted the wood bin filled with dry wood and kindling. Except for a coffee mug sitting next to the book on the table beside her, the room was spotless.

Feeling like an intruder in his own home, he hunkered down beside her.

He was glad that she'd changed back into her own clothes. The form-fitting long handles were far too alluring for him to continue to ignore. She now sported a pony tail, which made her look younger than her thirty years. A few stray wisps of dark hair fell loose to delicately frame her flawless features. Even the tiny cleft in her chin was perfectly perfect.

Physically Kacy Angelle could not be described as a classic beauty. Granted, she was blessed with the high cheekbones and slightly upturned nose he knew were coveted by most women, but it was her spirit, her constant battle of wills with him that intrigued him. And she was smart. She hadn't let her fear make her careless or helpless. From the beginning, she'd kept her wits about her, always seemed conscious of the fact that a wrong move on her part would be more deadly than no move at all.

My God, he thought, realizing how long it had been since he'd been attracted to a woman. *I admire her.*

Amazed by the track his thoughts had taken, he listened to her breathing, watched the steady rise and fall of her breasts. Which brought his gaze to the photo lying there.

The instant his fingers touched it, her eyes fluttered open. He expected her to pull away, to be frightened. Instead, she smiled up at him. A rush of exhilaration almost overwhelmed him.

'You're home,' she said, her voice slightly husky from sleeping. 'What? No more hostages?' Her smile broadened, then faded. The only thing that could have surprised him more would have been if she'd reached out and touched him — which was exactly what she did.

'You got a haircut.' Her fingers slid through his hair, then around his ear to caress his cheek.

Only those closest to Dan could get to him, emotionally speaking, but this innocent display of benevolence left him at a loss. He studied her for a long moment. What sort of feminine trick had she thought up while he was gone? *Don't be stupid*, he rebuked himself, knowing full well he was reacting exactly the way she wanted him to. He was tempted to call her bluff, to see just how far she was willing to go to get on his good side. That wouldn't be a smart move on his part, he warned himself immediately. Where this woman was concerned he didn't trust himself, and this definitely was a complication he could ill afford.

'It was driving me crazy,' he said, taking her hand in his. Without thinking, he ran his thumb across her palm. Her small gasp of surprise startled them both so much that he released her. In spite of his legs having gone weak on him, he managed to stand as he took the photo from her and placed it back where it belonged. Ray's face smiled at him. 'Have you eaten?' he asked brusquely, angry that she could make him forget even for a minute that his mission was far from over.

Kacy looked bewildered. 'No. I guess I forgot.' Her guileless expression weakened his reason again, then angered him anew.

'How can someone forget to eat?' He hoped that the growl in his voice would scare her off. She'd almost gotten to him. With stiff, automated movements, he started taking the canned goods out of the bags. He didn't hear Kacy approach until she stood beside him at the bar.

'Here, let me do that.' Gently she took the bag from him. 'You'd better get into some dry clothes.'

Shades of déjà vu. Last night he'd said pretty much the same thing to her, only instead of telling her to get *into* dry clothes, he'd ordered her *out* of her wet things. For reasons he couldn't fathom, that simple difference bothered him.

When he didn't respond, she said, 'You were gone a long time. I was getting — ' She stopped in midsentence.

'Worried about me?' he finished for her, secretly enjoying the flush of color that stained her face. 'Why, Kacy, I'm touched.'

He didn't think it possible for her face to flame brighter, but he was wrong. Now it was almost the exact shade of her sweater.

Her temper flared instantly. 'Don't flatter yourself.' Her spine was ramrod-stiff. 'If something had happened to you, I'd be up the proverbial creek.'

Obviously angered beyond the point of polite conversation, Kacy grabbed a can of chili and the can opener. Why had he done that? Hadn't he gone the extra mile to put her mind at rest? Now, he supposed, they were back to square one. He'd make it up to her later with his news of Mandy, he promised himself, leaving her to their meal while he showered and changed.

Kacy heard the bathroom door shut but continued to scrape chili from the can into a saucepan. Still fuming at her own stupidity, she turned on the burner, then began putting away the rest of the items in the bags. Crackers, catsup, a six-pack of Dr. Pepper, eggs, and more canned goods — corned beef hash, chili, and stew. And, to her surprise and delight, a box of cinnamon Teddy Grahams. The man had a sweet tooth!

In the other bag, she found a pink toothbrush, a Polaroid camera, still in its box, a pair of black leather loafers, a beige bra, and two pair of panties. She didn't dwell too long on how he'd known her underwear size, but a quick mental flash of him checking the tags inside her bra and panties as he moved them from the bathroom to the mantel this morning was the most logical explanation.

In the bottom of the sack, she came across a receipt for overnight mail delivery, a passbook for a savings account, today's edition of the Houston Chronicle — and a snapshot of Mandy and Mary in the Wee Care playground.

Tears welled up in Kacy's eyes,

forcing her to sit down at the bar. Mandy was wearing her favorite sneakers and the jacket Kacy had bought for her just last week. Her curly brown hair had been pulled into a high pony tail, leaving her soft, round face fully exposed to the eye of the camera. Normally, Kacy knew, Mandy would be romping in the middle of the playground action, but today she stood passively to one side, her small hand tightly clutching Mary's. Her daughter looked well, but she also looked sad and uncertain and frightened — much like she had two years ago in the airport lobby.

Kacy wiped away the tears that stained her cheeks. She knew that the photo had been snapped today because Bryan Calder was playing in the sandbox in the background. His mother brought him to Wee Care only on Tuesday afternoons while she kept her standing hairdresser's appointment. Dan Wilder had been less than twenty feet from Mandy sometime after school let out today.

The bathroom door opened and a spicy smell preceded Dan into the room. Now sporting clean jeans and the same chambray shirt Kacy had worn over her long johns, he bypassed her to stir the forgotten chili steaming on the stove.

'Just in time,' he said, his back to her. 'It was about to scorch.' When he faced her, she saw the regret on his face. 'I didn't mean for you to find that without explaining. Are you okay?'

Kacy had to clear her throat in order to speak. 'I . . . ' Emotion overwhelmed her. 'How did you know where — '

'They mentioned the name of your business on the news. Remember?' He spoke calmly, succinctly. 'And I figured your partner was the friend you called from Baytown. Mary, wasn't it?'

He still stood before the stove, giving Kacy time to regroup. She came to her feet and tucked the photo into the pocket of her jacket. Unconsciously she patted it as she spoke again.

'Yes, you figured right. I don't know why you took such a chance going back to Houston like that, but thank you.'

Suddenly he looked very uncomfortable. 'I had other things to take care of. It wasn't any trouble.' He busied himself by ladling chili into two bowls and placing them on the bar.

Kacy was over her surprise. 'No, I don't guess it would be much trouble.' She held up the brand-new camera. 'If you happen to have a camera with you.'

Dan straddled a stool on the kitchen side of the bar. 'There's a shopping center just two blocks from your day-care center,' he reminded her.

Kacy wanted to ask him if he'd spoken to Mandy or Mary. Had he told Mandy that her mommy was all right, reassured her that they would be together again in a few short days?

But mostly she wondered why he'd taken such a chance. Surely the authorities were watching her home and Wee Care. She glanced at the post office receipt and the passbook. He was one step ahead of her. He took both and stuffed them in his shirt pocket.

'Tell me a little about yourself,' he said, crumbling crackers into his chili. Next he shook a small amount of catsup into the bowl and stirred the concoction until crackers, chili, and catsup were well blended. 'So far all I know is that you're Kacy Angelle and you have a little girl named Mandy.' He looked up at her over his bowl. 'Oh, yeah, you're thirty years old and you're part owner in Wee Care Day Care. Cute name, by the way.' He took another bite, and Kacy scrunched up her nose in distaste.

'Under the circumstances,' she said, trying to ignore the globby mixture across from her, 'I think you know all you need to know.'

He grinned. 'Come on, Kacy. Humor me. Tell me what a rotten SOB your ex was, how adorable Mandy is. You know, work on my sympathy, get close to me. Then, zap! Make your move.' His eyes darkened and held hers. 'I think I like the idea of your making a move on me.'

In all their time together, she'd never gotten the impression that he deliberately wanted to make her uncomfortable. To the contrary, he'd gone out of his way to make her feel safe. Had she misjudged him completely? Was the snapshot of Mandy just a cruel maneuver to get her to let her guard down? She suddenly wished she hadn't put the knife away when she straightened the cutlery drawer.

'Hey,' he said, calling her attention back to his solemn face. 'Relax. I was teasing. You've got my word that I won't make a grab for you.'

His promise gave her cause for relief. 'Is that your word as a bank robber, a kidnapper, or a smart ass?' she shot back.

His Cheshire cat grin was instantaneous. 'Touché.' He took another bite, then idly stirred the chili around in his bowl again.

'How can you eat that mess?' Now that they were back on an even keel,

Kacy felt free to criticize. 'Didn't your mother teach you any manners?'

The gleam in his eyes told her she was in for it. 'My mother, God rest her soul, taught me that I could do anything I set my mind to, that children are our futures, and that I could crumble crackers in my chili.'

Kacy tried not to smile, but couldn't help herself. 'I suppose she also taught you how to cook biscuits and gravy.'

If she hadn't been watching so closely, she probably would have missed the light dim in his eyes before he lowered his lashes. 'No . . . ' he started, hesitated, then went on. 'My wife did that.'

'*You're* married?' She didn't mean to sound so incredulous, but that's how it came out. When he raised his gaze to hers, she could have sworn she saw pain lurking behind the cool greenness that bore into her.

'Am I *that* repulsive?'

Repulsive? All the man had to do was

look in the mirror to know that wasn't the case. He didn't wear a ring, but then lots of men didn't. Then she remembered his comment in the truck when he'd asked her if she was divorced. *There's a lot of that going around.*

'No, of course not.' Curiosity about the woman a man like him would love washed over her. 'What's your wife's name?' If he was divorced, it wouldn't hurt to know why. If he was still married, maybe it would work to her advantage. She didn't stop to analyze the sense of loss she felt at the thought that he might belong to another woman.

'Actually, I'm a widower.' He paused to sip from his tall glass of milk. 'Medicine's come a long way in eight years,' he said, standing and taking his dishes to the sink. 'You don't hear of too many people dying from pneumonia nowadays.' In a gesture she knew was unconscious, he rubbed the back of his neck. 'One of us didn't have a nap

174

earlier. I'm beat. Think I'll turn in early.'

With that, he followed pretty much the same routine as the night before. Kacy wanted to protest, tell him that she'd been alone all day, that she wanted to know about Mandy, to know how much longer he planned to keep her prisoner here. But she didn't. Instead, she did the dishes and took her turn in the bathroom.

Donning the long johns once again, she tiptoed around his bed roll, got her book, then crawled quietly into bed. Clicking on the lamp beside her, she opened the pages to chapter eight. On the floor, Dan shifted positions and fluffed his pillow, drawing Kacy's attention to him.

'Sorry,' she said. 'Is the light bothering you?'

'No, the floor's bothering me,' he groused, turning over again. 'And my feet are cold.'

Kacy laid the thriller aside. 'I don't mind sleeping on the floor.' Her offer was sincere, but she knew that he wouldn't take her up on it.

'No,' he answered, sitting up and folding his cover back. Sometime while she'd prepared for bed, he'd stripped down to nothing but the bottom half of a pair of thermal long johns. Standing, he bent over to push the cushions beneath his sleeping bag back together. The play of muscles across his back drew her attention like a magnet and she couldn't help noticing how nicely his rounded backside filled out the thermals or the way the material clung to his muscular thighs.

Her heart did crazy things inside her chest as he straightened and turned to face her. Quickly she averted her eyes before she embarrassed herself. He was beside the bed, rummaging through the trunk before she realized what he was doing. Clutching a clean pair of socks in his hand, he returned to his pallet, where he sat and put on the socks.

'That should help,' he said. 'Good night, Kacy, and I hope you're not too squeamish. That author gets pretty graphic with his violence.'

'If I can handle you, I think I can handle a work of fiction,' she answered with more bravado than she felt. She'd had to put the book down this afternoon, and it had been broad daylight.

Two chapters later, she put the book aside. How could a writer get into the villain's mind so well that the reader could be terrified of him, but at the same time feel an empathy that made the madman's motives seem normal?

This afternoon's nap hadn't been a good idea and she was paying the price for it now. There was no way she was going to sleep any time soon.

'Dan?'

There was a long pause before an exhausted 'Yeah?'

'I can't sleep,' she said, and hurried on before he could needle her about reading after he'd warned her. 'Can we talk?' She heard him yawn, then saw him roll onto his back.

'Sure,' he answered. 'Why not? We can talk about anything except Hawkins.'

Ground rules stated, she had to give the topic some thought. Mandy? No, she wasn't up to that. Mandy was being taken care of by someone who loved them both. With the exception of his relationship with Hawkins, he'd left the subject of himself wide open. Pretty dangerous ground, but it was better than talking about herself.

She knew exactly where she wanted to start. 'How long were you married?' She saw him stare at the ceiling.

'Seven years.'

'Were you happy?'

'She was a good woman.' He ran his fingers through his hair. 'Yeah,' he added after a moment. 'We were happy.'

'I'm sorry.'

He rolled his head to one side to look at her.

'No, I mean, I'm sorry about her death. Happy marriages are hard to find these days.'

'Sounds like you're talking from experience,' he turned the conversation to her. 'How long were you married?'

This wasn't what she'd had in mind at all, but fair was fair. Besides, she didn't have to tell him her life's story. 'Ted and I were married just over a year.'

'Hardly had a chance to get to know each other,' he observed through another yawn.

'Long enough to know that I'd made the biggest mistake an eighteen-year-old could make.'

The room grew quiet again. 'Must not have been too bad. You did it again.'

She hadn't the faintest notion as to what he meant. 'What?'

'Your little girl can't be more than six or seven. Someone somewhere along the way must have made you forget about good old Ted.'

He certainly figured fast, she thought, beginning to regret starting this. 'No, I never remarried.' Realizing how that sounded, she went on to explain, 'I'm in the process of adopting Mandy.'

Again he ruffled his hair. 'The law's come a long way, too,' he said, sitting up. 'Single parents adopting nowadays. That's great.' Firelight flickered across the shadows that hid his face. 'Ellie wasn't able to have children. We were turned down time and time again because — well, Ellie was a frail woman. She was sick a lot.'

Kacy heard in his wistful tone that he'd slipped back in time. Instead of interrupting to ask more questions, she turned out her light and lay back on her pillow.

'You're an attractive woman with a lot to offer a man,' he said after a moment, his voice carrying softly across the room. 'Why didn't you ever remarry?'

The abuse she'd suffered at Ted's hands was a subject she never discussed. Only Mary knew about the miscarriage that had left her barren. On one hand, Kacy wanted to tell Dan about it; on the other, she refused to let the past out to hurt her again.

'None of my business, right?' He sounded like he'd come to some conclusions of his own, although he didn't voice them.

'No, it's not that,' she answered. 'It's just not something I'm comfortable talking about.' It was close enough to the truth that she hoped he wouldn't push.

' 'Nuff said.'

She was glad that he'd dropped it, but she still wanted to talk. 'Dan?'

'Yeah?'

'What's the Q stand for?'

'Back to me, are we?'

'Looks like. Is it Quinton?'

'I wish.'

'Then what?'

He chuckled and the sound warmed Kacy through and through. 'Would you believe Qute?'

'Hardly, but that's real cute.'

'I thought so.'

'Seriously. What's it for?'

'Give me a break, Kacy,' he said. 'You don't need to know everything. Besides, it'll give you something to think about.'

'Yeah, sure. Like I don't already have enough on my mind.' She meant it to be lighthearted, but the silence that followed made her want to take back her words.

'You'll never know how sorry I am about that,' he finally answered.

So they were back to square one. 'Dan?'

'What?' Now he was starting to sound irritated.

'Who's the man in the picture with you?'

He took so long to answer that she knew she'd regret asking the question.

'He was my brother.'

8

Rest eluded Dan long after Kacy was sleeping soundly. The combination of the steady downpour outside and the crackling fire next to him should have helped him sleep. It didn't, though, and he punched up his pillow again and tried to settle in more comfortably. Restless and tired of trying to fall asleep, he tossed from his side to his back, where he stayed for all of five seconds before rolling to his other side. Nothing seemed to help. Suddenly he found himself wishing she'd wake up and say his name again.

Their talk earlier hadn't amounted to much, but he'd learned more from what she hadn't told him than the little she'd volunteered. The most revealing thing was that her marriage had been a disaster. Something had happened all those years ago, something that continued to haunt her, although she did her best to deny it. Just as he tried to deny the guilt he felt for Ray's death.

Intellectually Dan knew he had nothing to feel guilty about. In his heart, though, he felt that if Ray'd had more confidence in himself, hadn't believed that he would never measure up to Dan, he'd have come to Dan for help instead of getting mixed up with Hawkins and his business loan scam.

Frustrated, Dan flung the top layer of the sleeping bag aside and sat up. Damn, he needed a drink. He came to his feet and reached for his shirt, which was draped over the back of the recliner, slipped it on without bothering to button it, then padded across the hardwood floor to the kitchen. He knew every nook and cranny of the adjoining rooms, so he didn't bother turning on a light. He found the bottle of bourbon on the top shelf in the cupboard.

A soft whimper from the den reached

his ears. He placed the unopened bottle on the bar and sought Kacy's sleeping form across the darkened room.

She tossed fretfully under the blankets, and her feet were uncovered again. He smiled. It seemed she wasn't content unless they were out in the open. He was just the opposite. If his size tens were cold, he was miserable. His smile faded when she cried out in her sleep. Four easy strides and he was sitting beside her on the bed.

How it happened he wasn't sure, but suddenly she was in his arms, clinging so tightly to him that he couldn't have pried her loose if he'd wanted to.

'It's all right, baby,' he crooned softly into her hair. Until this very moment, he hadn't realized how badly he'd wanted to hold her. His hand cupped the back of her head to hold her tenderly against his bare shoulder. The feel of her body trembling in his arms, the sound of her soft sobbing drew out every protective instinct in him. But more than that, she felt right in his embrace, filled a void he hadn't known existed until that very moment. Would he be strong enough to let her go if she tried to pull away?

'He wouldn't stop . . . I couldn't get away from him . . . ' Her muffled words mingled with the tears he felt on his skin. He found the answer to his question when her hands came up between their bodies to push against him. Reluctantly he released her and she withdrew a few inches that felt to him like miles.

'I'm sorry,' she apologized through sniffles. 'It was just so real.'

His first thought was that reading the book before falling asleep had triggered a nightmare. He'd tried to warn her about the author's penchant for graphic violence. But when he leaned back and looked into her face, he knew that wasn't the case.

'This wasn't just a bad dream, was it?' He cupped her chin, then tilted it up so that he could see her eyes. 'It was a memory.'

Whether she denied it or not, Dan knew that he had hit on the truth — that son of a bitch of a husband had hurt her, had *physically* hurt her.

Kacy sniffed brokenly, then lowered her head. But not before he saw the struggle waging inside her. If she confided too much, she would feel exposed, vulnerable. She had too much pride for that, he knew.

'It was a nightmare.' Her soft whisper neither affirmed nor denied his allegation. She surprised him next by leaning back into his embrace, accepting all the support he was willing to give. And, he realized in amazement, he was willing to give all that was in him. Not only because in her arms his own pain and regrets were momentarily assuaged, but, to his utter dismay, because he had come to care for her.

The contact of their bodies was the sweetest and most disturbing thing Dan had ever experienced. Where, he wondered as his hands explored the gentle curve from her waist to the small of her back, had his control gone? The thin barrier of cloth that kept flesh from touching flesh seemed only to heighten his awareness of her breasts pressing against his bare chest. He breathed in the scent of her freshly shampooed hair, and then his lips sought the sensitive hollow just below her ear. He felt her trembling subside, and she turned to him, her lips finding his and meeting his ardor without restraint.

She didn't protest when his fingers grazed the soft swell of breast on their way to the buttons of her long johns. But when her hands covered his, he thought she was having second thoughts.

With supreme effort, he waited for her to make the decision that would bind them together even after all this was over.

Tentatively her fingers caressed each of his before trailing up the length of his arms to push his shirt off his shoulders. He lowered his hands for her to remove the shirt. The only physical contact between them now was that of their lips — nipping, tasting, testing each other's reactions to this unexpected intimacy.

Dan heard a soft moan as her lips parted for the gentle plunder of his tongue. So caught up was he in the magic they were creating together that he wasn't sure if the sound came from him or from her. Her fingers glided over his shoulders, across his chest, and down his stomach. His own hands were not idle. The buttons on her long johns fell away, baring her to the waist, and he had to see her. He withdrew to gaze down at her.

She was a dream bathed in firelight. Her lips were softly swollen from their kiss, and her breasts, full and perfect with their budding tips, seemed to cry out for his touch. Her eyes, when she opened them to look up at him, were deep-brown pools of confusion shining bright with tears.

Just as he knew that she was his for the taking, he also knew that he couldn't have her like this.

'Dan?' The quiver of uncertainty in her voice reinforced his resolve.

'Go back to sleep, baby,' he said, helping her with the buttons. Then, feigning a more light-hearted note, he added, 'I allow only one bad dream a night, so you can rest easy now. You know where I am if you need me.' He stood and would have walked away if she hadn't reached for his hand.

'I need you now.' Her voice was soft, yet strong in conviction. Her dark gaze refused to waver.

Never could he remember his will-power being tested like this. But until he was sure that he wasn't putting his needs before hers, he wouldn't do anything to cause her regret.

'You don't need me, Kacy. You want me. They're two entirely different things.'

She moved to the center of the bed and pushed the blankets back in a silent invitation. 'Not necessarily.' She wasn't making this easy. 'What's the matter? Am I scaring you now?'

Dan swallowed the oath that rose in his throat. 'Kacy, you're too vulnerable right now to know what you want or need,' he argued gently, barely recognizing the husky voice he heard as his own. He tugged his hand free, then left her before his selfcontrol dissolved.

Somehow facing that empty sleeping bag was the last thing he wanted. He found his way to the recliner and slumped into it with a weary sigh. In his heart he knew he'd done the right thing, but his body ached from the betrayal of his noble intentions.

The storm outside raged on, and he didn't hear her approach until she stood next to him. He tensed at the warmth of her feather-light touch on his shoulder.

'You're a good man, Daniel Qute Wilder.' She slipped onto his lap and covered them both with the blanket she'd brought with her from her bed.

'All I want is for you to hold me.' She

rested her head on his shoulder. 'I need you to hold me.' She sighed contentedly. 'And we're not in the bed, so you can stop trying to be so brave and steadfast.'

She wasn't giving him a chance to refuse. Again he breathed in the intoxicating smell of her, and he didn't have it in him to object when she snuggled closer. The message had been sent and received: They each needed physical comfort without the complication of sexual intimacy. What a wonderful discovery for both of them.

For the first time in weeks, Dan drifted into a peaceful slumber — and without the aid of alcohol.

* * *

Michaelson thumbed through the stack of messages he found on his desk until he saw the name that had been on his mind more often than not of late. According to the memo, the call had come in yesterday afternoon at five-fifteen.

For the first time in days, the morning sun sliced through the venetian blinds to fall in a striped pattern across his desk. He dialed the phone number scrawled along the bottom of the message and waited while it rang four, five, then six times.

'Wee Care Day Care.'

He recognized her voice immediately. 'Ms. Martin, this is Special Agent Michaelson. How can I help you this morning?' He grimaced at the Joe-Friday tone that automatically came out of his mouth.

'Oh, yes, Detective Michaelson.' She sounded breathless, and he had to consciously push aside the image that flashed through his mind of her lying beside him in his big old bed. No doubt she would be soft and cuddly, utterly feminine, everything he wanted in a woman . . .

The chatter of children in the background brought him back to the real world. 'Have I caught you at a bad time?' he had the presence of mind to ask.

'No.' She laughed. 'Well, yes, but around here it's as good a time as any. Can you hold on while I change telephones?'

'No problem.'

He waited while she put him on hold. He was just getting into the second verse of 'Somewhere Over the Rainbow' when she picked up on another line.

'That's much better,' she said with an audible sigh that made him smile. Then she was serious again. 'Something happened yesterday that — ' She stopped suddenly, then went on. 'I feel a little silly about this, but I can't get it out of my mind.'

Michaelson took his pen in hand and leaned forward. He'd learned a long time ago never to discount a woman's intuition. 'I'm listening.'

'The weather's been so bad lately that when the sun came out for a few hours yesterday, we took the children out into the play yard.' She paused again, further piquing his interest. 'Anyway, I saw a pickup — a black pickup — parked across the street, and there was a man walking back to it. I hadn't noticed him before, but I got the impression that he'd been at our fence. He had a camera in his hand, and, well, it just seemed odd to me.'

Pickups in Texas were as common as tight-fitting Levis and cowboy boots, but details were essential to his profession, and Michaelson was very good at his job. He jotted down everything Mary told him.

'You think this might have something to do with Miss Angelle's disappearance?'

Mary didn't answer right away. When she did, Michaelson heard the mixture of doubt and helplessness in her voice. 'I don't know. I just want so badly to help.'

'Did you happen to get a license number?' Long shot that it was, some things Michaelson asked from years of experience.

'Yes.' She gave him the number, which he quickly scribbled on his note pad. 'I hope I'm not sending you on a wild-goose chase. We have several children here whose parents are going through divorces,' she went on. 'It could have been something as innocent as a father who simply wanted a snapshot of his child.'

A knock sounded on Michaelson's office door. He frowned and looked up to see a UPS driver being ushered in. The man clad in brown placed a small package in the middle of the desk, then shoved a clipboard under Michaelson's pen.

'We can't afford to overlook even the slightest clue, Ms. Martin.' He regretted that the G-man in him had resurfaced, but he had an audience. He signed on line four, then watched the driver close the door on his way out. 'I'll have this checked out and get back to you when I know more.' He didn't *have* to get back to her on anything. He had the information, and if it turned out to be anything at all, he would follow up on it. But it was as good an excuse as any to see her again.

They said their good-byes and Michaelson turned his attention to the package before him. No return address, he noted, but its origin was Beaumont. Carefully he opened it to find two computer disks and a note inside.

He unfolded the slip of paper and read: *Michaelson*, it began in a bold handwriting. *Ray trusted you. I guess I have to now. The woman's okay. I can't let her go until it's safe.*

That there wasn't a signature didn't surprise him. Any doubts he'd had before were laid to rest now. He knew who he was dealing with. He glanced down at the notes on his desk. Gut instinct told him that Mary's information would confirm it. He purposely hadn't gotten a description of the man near Wee Care yesterday. Another excuse to get back with her later today.

The only problem Dan and Kacy experienced during the remainder of the night was that she kept kicking the cover off her feet, which left his uncovered as well. Finally at dawn, he had gently roused her to tuck her back into her own bed, where she slept for several more hours.

Now that they'd had their morning and noon meals, Kacy was restless and cranky. She'd tried looking at her captivity as a mini-vacation where she didn't have to be up at five each morning in order to be at Wee Care by six-thirty. She had no makeup with her, so her morning toilet consisted of changing out of the long johns and into her own clothes, washing her face, brushing her teeth, and pulling her hair back into a neat pony tail. Without her curling iron and hair spray, it seemed the only way to keep it out of her face.

Conversation between them had been scant when existent, relating to subjects as mundane as how Kacy wanted her eggs or if the shoes fit her properly. Once she broached the subject of how long Dan planned to keep her prisoner, and he stalked out the door.

Never one to leave something unfinished, she'd whiled away three hours to finish the horror novel while Dan restocked their supply of wood from the cords stacked behind the cabin and cleaned the guns he kept in the gun cabinet. Now she was bored. Common sense warned her not to provoke him with more questions, but if she had to stay cooped up inside these four walls much longer, she would scream.

'Feel like getting out for a while?' Dan asked as if he'd read her mind. He sat on the sofa and pulled on a pair of knee-high rubber boots. She was glad he'd taken the initiative in breaking the silence he'd imposed on them. 'Looks like it's going to be a great day.'

Kacy wanted to jump for joy and throw her arms around him, but, of course, she didn't. It was early afternoon, and she couldn't help wondering if he was as relieved as she was that neither of them had mentioned their nocturnal encounter. The dream had been especially hellish, which was the only acceptable excuse she could come up with for inviting him into her bed. A rush of warmth flowed through her as she recalled how bold she had been. Thank goodness he'd had the insight to realize that she had reached out to him in a moment of weakness. Sometime during the day she would find the right time to tell him how grateful she was.

Remembering the nightmare, she shivered inwardly. The dreams had come less and less often over the years; now she suffered them on an average of once a month. She had yet to figure out what had triggered the memories of Ted this time. Possibly it had been their midnight conversation, or the conscienceless villain in the thriller, or the fact that until that afternoon she'd been as frightened of Dan as she had been of

200

her ex-husband. More than likely, she finally concluded, it had been a combination of all three.

'I have to make sure the truck's okay.' Dan's voice broke into her thoughts. 'The river should have crested during the night, and with all the rain that's fallen, it's probably up to its headlights in swamp water.' He stood at the bar, tucking his wallet into his hip pocket, then his shirttail into his jeans. 'Leave the lamp on. In case it's late when we get back, it'll help guide us in.'

The idea of getting back into the canoe was a frightening prospect, but, as things stood, it was either that or cabin fever. Quickly slipping on her new shoes, she grabbed her jacket and followed him outside.

Indeed, it was a glorious day. The reading on the outdoor thermometer was seventy degrees, which didn't really surprise Kacy. Winter in the Gulf Coast region was unpredictable, at best — cold and wet one day, warm and balmy the next.

The sun smiled down from high overhead, bathing Kacy's upturned face with the first rays of warmth she'd felt in a long, long while. Mary would have the children outside today, she thought, missing Mandy with every fiber of her being. In her mind's eye, she visualized the child running and laughing with her best friends, Haylee and Brittany. Tears stung her eyes, and she wiped them away with fingers that were suddenly unsteady. She sensed, rather than saw, Dan's gaze on her.

'Nothing like it, is there?' he said, lifting his own face toward the sky. As badly as she missed Mandy, she couldn't find it in her heart to think ill of him. From the very first time she'd laid eyes on him, she sensed that he was motivated by something much more elemental than greed. Watching him at this moment, she saw no trace of the ruffian who had assaulted Hawkins or the outlaw who had kidnapped her. This was a man at peace with nature and his Maker.

The grin he flashed her took her breath away. 'Piggyback you to the boat?' he asked, giving her his back. When she didn't answer, he glanced over his shoulder. 'There's lots of mud and water between us and the river. Wouldn't want to lose another pair of shoes, would you?'

Put that way, it sounded reasonable enough. She stood on the top step and climbed aboard. His strong arms wrapped around each leg to keep her securely in place as he sloshed toward the overturned canoe.

The ground was as muddy as he'd said it was, but he found a spot dry enough for her to stand on while he righted the small vessel, then dragged it into deeper water. He came back, swung her into his arms, and neatly deposited her in the middle of the boat.

'You'd have a better view from the front seat, but if you're still uneasy, sit just like you did the other night,' he told her. 'A word of warning, though. Don't grab hold of anything outside the boat, even if it feels unsteady. It could cause us to turn over. Just relax and enjoy the ride. Let me handle anything that happens.'

She had no interest in the sightseeing, so she took his suggestion. Positioning the boat cushion in the middle of the canoe's floor, she prepared herself for the trip.

With an economy of movement, the canoe glided from the shallows into the swiftly moving current of the Sabine. The quiet that enveloped them once they were on the water was eerie at first, but in time Kacy realized that it wasn't quiet at all. Small sounds, insect and bird calls, the chattering of squirrels scampering from treetop to treetop, the buzz of a dragonfly skimming the water's surface, reached her ears, and she, too, began to feel at peace, not only with her surroundings, but with herself as well.

Until a loud bellow that sounded like a lovesick cow shattered the serenity. Kacy jerked upright, her hands clutching the sides of the canoe so tightly that her knuckles felt strained.

'It's okay,' Dan assured her with a chuckle. 'It's just a bull frog. See, there he goes.' He raised his paddle to point toward a log that had gotten entangled in a floating pile of river debris.

Kacy glimpsed the brownish-green amphibian just as it lunged into the water, upsetting the log and dumping two small turtles into the murky river in the process.

'Sunbathing after all this cold weather,' he explained. 'Hard to believe something so small can sound that formidable. Good eating, though.'

Small? That was the biggest frog Kacy had ever seen. Its legs were the size of a well-fed chicken's.

Behind her, Dan's paddle began slapping water again, and each time the noise stopped, she felt the canoe being guided past a brush top, or a fallen tree, or a stump. Eventually she began to relax. The man obviously was an experienced outdoorsman.

After so many weeks of foul weather, the sky overhead was remarkably blue and dotted with fluffy patches of white. Far in the distance, hanging in resplendent glory over the river, was the most magnificent rainbow Kacy had ever seen. The arc was a masterpiece of colors — reds, blues, yellows — made more spectacular by the contrast of blue sky and the browns and greens of earth, water, and foliage. She was enthralled, for what had appeared forbidding and untamed in the dark was a wonderland in daylight. Even the trees dripping with Spanish moss were a delight to behold.

Lining what should have been the riverbank, but was underwater now, were magnificent cypress trees, their knobby knees protruding out of the water at their bases like darling children. Willows bowed in graceful deference to the mighty red oaks and sprawling live oaks. Deeper into the thicket, she saw Chinese tallow trees and small dogwoods that would grace the forest with myriad white blossoms in March and April. It was another world, one untouched by civilization.

'I think she's made another conquest,' Dan said in a reverent whisper.

'She?' Kacy asked in kind, afraid that something as simple as the sound of her voice would break the mystical spell.

'Mother Nature,' he answered, and Kacy heard the awe, the respect, he held for this place. 'It's God's creation, unmarred by man's hand. You've already heard Him talking to you through the creatures who live here. Close your eyes and feel His sweet breath on your face.'

Unhesitatingly she did as he said. A faint breeze wafted about them, and gradually she was filled with a sense of peacefulness she had never before known.

They traveled without talking, and sooner than Kacy would have liked, she saw a splash of black in a stand of trees. The pickup was facing the opposite direction, she noticed, thinking that he'd readied it for a quick getaway.

The canoe dragged bottom as Dan skillfully maneuvered it through the trees and foliage. Then, without so much as rocking the boat, he got out and slogged his way through the thigh-high backwater, leaving Kacy where she sat.

She watched him circle the vehicle, saw him carefully inspect each tire, then open the door. Water spilled out of the cab and he climbed in to try the engine. It chugged and spit a few times, but it didn't start. Quickly checking under the hood, he uttered a few choice words she didn't hear too often. A scowl wrinkled his tanned forehead beneath his weathered hat as he trudged back to her.

'As long as the weather holds and the water continues to drop, I think it'll be okay here. But it'll take me a little while to get it back in running order,' he told her, reaching out for her hand. 'You'll be more comfortable in the back of the truck.'

She came to her feet, and he swept her up and out of the canoe. Neither of them had bothered putting on the coats they brought along, and the physical contact between them brought back memories of the night before. Kacy prayed that the rush of warmth flowing through her wouldn't color her face. Blushing wasn't her style any more than having heart palpitations over an outlaw.

Seeming not to notice his effect on her, Dan lowered the tailgate, then placed her with great care in the cargo bed. He took off his western hat and placed it on her head.

'Not much chance of your getting a sunburn, but let's not chance it.' Lithely he bounded up beside her to rummage through the tool chest butted up against the cab. Unlocking it, he took the tools he needed, then leapt to the ground to go about his chore.

The sun felt good on her face, so she removed the misshapen hat, placed it on the wheel hub, where she propped her head and promptly dozed off.

The next thing she heard was Dan's voice. 'Okay, sleeping beauty, we're all set.'

Groggy, Kacy sat up. She had no idea how long she'd slept, but, although it was still daylight, she didn't see the sun in the sky. At last she found it lurking behind the trees to the west.

'If we get a move on, we'll make it back to the camp around dusk.' He extended his hand to help her slide to the end of the tailgate. Once there, her legs dangling over the edge, she didn't move into his arms, nor did he reach for her.

Freeze-framed in time, neither of them spoke or moved. Kacy searched his face, again falling under the spell of his hypnotic green eyes. The squiggle of crow's-feet there drew her attention from his penetrating gaze before she took in each detail of his features. How had she missed the tiny white scar that streaked just above the fullness of his upper lip? And in the daylight his hair was as dark as her own.

The seconds that passed were in no way awkward or embarrassing. To the contrary, it was a moment shared, a moment to remember.

And it was the perfect time to say what had been on her mind every waking moment since last night.

'I haven't thanked you . . . ' she began, wincing at the crack in her voice. Determined to get it out, she forced her gaze to meet his squarely. 'About last night . . . ' This wasn't as easy as she'd hoped it would be. 'I . . . haven't had one that bad in a lot of years. Thank you for recognizing how frightened I was and for not taking advantage of the situation.'

He listened without speaking, which she was grateful for, but then he raised his hand and caressed her cheek. His touch seemed to awaken every dormant nerve ending in every fiber of her being, and she had to fight for control of her thoughts.

'I . . . I . . . ' she stammered, angry

with herself for being distracted when his hand slipped behind her neck, his fingers splaying through her hair to gently hold her immobile. 'I put you in a terrible position,' she plunged on. 'And,' she added, her voice weakening, 'I scared myself.'

Dan's soft chuckle was the last thing she expected. 'Not half as bad as you scared me.' He inched closer, wedged himself snugly between her legs.

Images of his shirtless torso crashed into her brain at the same time her hands came to rest on his chest. Her eyes fastened on the pulse at the base of his throat, then dipped lower to the dark tangle of hair peeking out of his shirt. She lowered her lashes, hoping to blot out each glimpse she'd had of his powerfully built body in the past three days. The spicy fragrance she'd come to associate with no one but Dan clung to him, assailed her senses and her composure. She had no idea that she wasn't breathing until he softly said her name.

She opened her eyes. His gaze held hers, wouldn't allow her to look away. Then, with tantalizing deliberation, he lowered his head to hers, lightly grazed her mouth with his lips, nuzzled her chin, then came back to claim the kiss he'd toyed with earlier. Her tongue answered the challenge of his, boldly tasted and tempted him with a wantonness she was sure would shock her later.

She heard him groan, then felt him retreat.

Never had she felt so deserted.

He smiled down at her, not a taunting smile of victory, but one of tenderness and understanding. 'As much as I'd love to pursue this, I have to be practical.' He stroked her cheek with the back of his fingers. 'It'll take us twice as long to paddle back upriver, so we'd better be on our way.'

This time when he took her in his arms, she gave herself over to the feeling and reveled in the closeness of their bodies. Too soon, they were at the canoe.

'If it'll help us make better time,' she offered, 'I'll paddle, too.'

He must have sensed that she was telling him that she trusted him, not only with her safety on the water, but with her emotions because he embraced her with an urgency that surprised her. This time, his reluctance to release her was painfully obvious.

He gave her a steadying hand to the seat in the front, where he handed her the extra paddle. Shoving off, he gave her a few instructions that she followed without error, and then they were on their way.

True to his word, they reached the camp shortly after nightfall. In the two hours they'd been on the water, she'd had time for soul-searching. When she saw the light shining from the cabin, she felt a pang of panic. She was bright enough to realize that with everything that had passed between them, the ground rules had changed. But how?

She was still his captive, at his mercy. What would he expect from her now?

She had been with only one man in her life, and that had been well over eleven years ago. Since then, she had never been able to trust enough to go beyond casual dating. But when Dan held her, kissed her, the past became a distant blur. Still, she wasn't sure if she was ready for an intimate relationship. Would she be the disappointment to him that she'd been to Ted? She couldn't take the chance.

Settling her on the bottom step, he held her at arm's length. 'This afternoon proved something to me.' He was more serious than she'd ever seen him. 'What happened last night wasn't an illusion created by need. We weren't just two desperate people reaching out for whatever comfort we could take from each other.' He leaned forward to rest his forehead against hers. 'Something wonderful has come from all this craziness.'

What he was saying to her now

should have helped, but it didn't. She couldn't let him bare his soul like this when she was riddled with so many doubts.

'Dan — '

Without warning, the door opened and a stranger stepped out onto the porch. The light from inside glowed brightly behind him, casting his massive form in a stark silhouette.

Relief washed over her like a tidal wave. She was saved — from being held captive and from having to face her feelings for her captor.

9

The stranger grinning down at them looked to be a bear of a man. Tall and muscular, his presence dominated the small front porch. A dark, scraggly beard covered his face, and Kacy recognized the shirt he wore as the one Dan had worn the day he whisked her away from the bank. His dark hair was wet and uncombed.

'I was startin' to git worried 'bout you, Wilder.' If she didn't do it now, Kacy thought, screwing up her courage, she might not have another chance. She started to take the second step, but Dan's fingers bit into her arm.

'This isn't someone you want to get mixed up with,' he said low enough that only she heard. Intuitively she knew that Dan had sensed that she was on the verge of blurting out the kidnapping story. She wanted nothing more than to do just that, to save herself from having to deal with her feelings for Dan, but his tone and his rigid stance made her heed his warning. Until she was certain about whom to trust, she would watch and listen, then make up her own mind.

In a move that was none too discreet, Dan placed himself between her and the intruder. 'What are you doing here, Broussard?' He reminded her of the male of any species warning an interloper that trespassing would not be tolerated.

Broussard's grin faded. 'That ain't very neighborly of you.' Clearly he wasn't happy with the directness of Dan's question. 'Why don't you git the little lady in outta the cold, and I'll tell you all 'bout it.' He stepped back inside to let them enter.

With twilight, the temperature had dropped and the fire blazing in the fireplace was a welcome sight. She should have been warmed by it. Instead, the animosity she sensed between the two men sent a chill that had nothing to do with the weather slicing through her.

Dan discarded his coat and hat to face Broussard with a grim expression. 'I asked you a question.'

Now that they were in better light, Kacy saw that the stranger wasn't as huge as she'd first thought. He and Dan were about the same size and build, although Broussard was a little thicker around the middle.

Broussard ran a beefy hand through his damp, tousled hair. 'Overturned my pirogue late this afternoon and lost it in the current.' A smile that missed being cordial by miles spread across his face. 'Sure was glad to find your place unlocked. Didn't see your truck out back, though.'

Dan's reluctance to answer was as obvious as his displeasure at finding Broussard in his cabin. 'I managed to get it out before the roads flooded.'

'So you're boatin' in and out,' Broussard prodded with a glance at

Kacy. 'You leave it at Fontenot's Landing?'

'Not exactly.' Dan eased toward Kacy to stand beside her in front of the fire. 'When did you get back to these parts?'

It would have been apparent to anyone with one good eye that there was no love lost between these two. Even so, Kacy wondered at Dan's evasiveness.

' 'Bout a week ago.' Broussard took a seat on one of the bar stools. He'd helped himself to the canned beef stew and he took a bite, then wiped his mouth on his shirt sleeve. He'd also broken the seal on the Wild Turkey. He turned up his glass, and his Adam's apple bobbed with each swig. 'New Orleans is a good place to lay low, but me and the law there didn't git along any better'n me and the law anywhere.' He said it with pride as he took another bite.

'Sorry to hear 'bout Ray,' he said around the mouthful, his condolence lacking any sincerity at all. 'I know what it's like not to have any family left. Been on my own since '88.' Again he glanced at Kacy. 'Ain't you gonna introduce the lady?'

As looks went, Broussard wasn't bad; in fact, he was handsome in a sinister sort of way. Still, there was something about the way he leered at her that made her skin feel like it was being peeled off her body. Suddenly she was grateful that Dan had stopped her outside before she made a terrible mistake. Attractive or not, Broussard was not a man to be trusted.

The silence that charged the air put Kacy's nerves on edge. 'I'm Dan's friend, Kacy Angelle.' She edged closer to Dan, hoping that Broussard would pick up on the subtle, though false, implication that there was more to their relationship.

'John Broussard.' He showed his teeth again in that grin Kacy had already labeled as treacherous. 'But my friends call me *Big* John.' His emphasis on the word *big* turned the grin from treacherous to lascivious in less than a heartbeat.

'What do you want, Broussard?' Dan didn't bother to disguise his dislike for the man.

Broussard's features were a study in control. 'It's too late to go lookin' for my pirogue tonight. Thought you'd give me a hand at first light.'

Dan wrapped one arm around Kacy's waist, reinforcing her earlier inference that they were more than friends. She welcomed the gesture. It felt good. It felt right. It felt safe. 'That dugout of yours could be in Sabine Lake by now.'

'Yeah, I know. But I figure if we don't come 'cross it hung up somewhere before Deweyville, you can just put me off at my place.' Broussard glanced from Dan to Kacy, then back. 'My game bag and best shotgun were tied down in that boat. Sure would like to have 'em back. 'Specially the Remington. It's been in my family since day one.'

Again Dan hesitated, prompting Broussard to come to his feet. 'The temperature's supposed to drop below forty tonight. You ain't turnin' me out just 'cause you got *company*, are you?' Kacy had never heard the word company sound so sleazy.

Several times during the day, she had wished Mandy could be with her to enjoy the river trip, especially the rainbow. She had been appalled that she couldn't remember if the child had ever seen one. Now, looking at the unsavory stranger glaring at Dan, she was relieved that Mandy was safe with Mary.

Kacy could see that Broussard's plea hadn't fallen on deaf ears; although Dan didn't like it, he had no choice but to help the stranded man.

'No, I'm not turning you out,' he said. 'Quarters are cramped, though, so you'll have to sleep on the floor.'

Kacy jerked her head up to stare at Dan in astonishment. If Big John Broussard slept on the floor, where did that leave Dan Wilder sleeping?

'I got no problem with that.' Broussard dug into his stew again. 'There's plenty on the stove and it's still hot. Help yourselves.'

Dan gave Kacy a squeeze of reassurance before he released her. 'You hungry?' he asked as though nothing was amiss.

Kacy felt her ire rising. 'I think we'd better talk.'

'Later.' He tried to walk away.

She laid a restraining hand on his arm. 'When?' she whispered. 'Before or after you crawl into my bed?'

Placing his hand over hers, he looked her squarely in the eye. 'It's *my* bed, and I said we'd talk later.'

Supper was an unhurried affair, with Dan and Big John each having second helpings of the stew Kacy found hard to swallow. In time, Broussard drew Dan into polite conversation, and she listened to the hunter's tale of having killed more than the legal limit of ducks before the small boat he kept referring to as a pirogue tipped over.

She sipped her Dr. Pepper and watched Dan's expression, listened to his carefully neutral comments on Broussard's yarn until suddenly it dawned on her: Dan was humoring his uninvited, unwanted guest. What she didn't know was why.

Broussard continued his account with a belch he chose not to acknowledge. Finally winding down, he added that he hoped the weather would stay cold enough that the birds wouldn't be rank by the time they found the pirogue.

Tiring of the masculine prattle, she started clearing away their dishes. The weight of the bowls in her hands caused her to wince in pain. Quickly putting the utensils down, she looked at her palms.

Dan didn't miss the pain on her face. 'Let's see,' he said, taking both hands and leading her to better light. A scowl creased his tanned forehead, drew his dark eyebrows together. 'Why didn't you tell me you were getting blisters?'

'Because I didn't realize it myself.'

'They don't look too bad, but I'll get the first-aid kit.' He was up and headed for the bathroom before she could protest that they were fine. She saw him pull up short at the door, then turn to glower at Broussard in disgust.

A sheepish look crept across Broussard's face. 'Sorry 'bout that. I didn't git a chance to straighten up.'

'Now's as good a time as any.' Dan minced no words as he stepped over the pile of soggy clothes that cluttered the floor of the small bathroom. He found the first-aid kit in the cabinet under the lavatory, then Broussard met him in the doorway.

'Hope you don't mind me borrowin' your clothes, but mine's wetter'n a fifteen-year-old's dreams.'

Dan's green gaze darkened. 'Watch your foul mouth, Broussard, or you'll find yourself sleeping on the porch.' He stood his ground, forcing Broussard to step around him.

Kacy could feel the color in her face. She was a grown woman and as such she could handle most things. Swearing was one thing; vulgarity was another.

Dan straddled the stool next to her and opened the kit. 'Now where's that damned card that tells you how to tend to different injuries?'

'Dan, you're not sleeping in my bed,' she whispered, deadly serious.

He deserted his search for the instruction card and glanced up at her. 'Oh, you mean to say that you prefer *Big* John?' The roguish glimmer dancing in his eyes made them appear greener. 'You know, I think he likes you, too.'

Kacy tried to yank her hands free, but he held on to them. 'Don't be ridiculous.' How could he tease her like that? She wasn't an expert on men, by any means, but she'd seen and heard enough to know that Broussard was no better than an animal.

'It says here,' Dan said, changing the subject by referring to the chart he finally found, 'not to break the blisters, just to cleanse them. We don't even have to bandage them unless they break.' He opened a bottle of hydrogen peroxide, then, with great care, dabbed at the blisters with a saturated cotton ball. The blisters themselves were puffy-white, the skin around them an angry red, but they didn't really hurt; they were only tender.

The last thing she expected him to do was bend down and place a kiss in each palm, but that's exactly what he did. That they were discussing something as important as sleeping arrangements was momentarily forgotten.

Each day at work she kissed dozens of 'boo-boo's,' but she couldn't remember the last time someone, other than Mandy, had cared enough to do something so touching for her. He raised his head and stroked the area again with the cotton ball, then checked his handiwork. They both knew he held her hands a little longer than was

228

necessary. His large sun-browned hands closed over hers and his thumb caressed her fingertips, sending unexpected tremors through her that she prayed he couldn't feel.

'So soft,' he murmured, almost reverently. 'So small.'

He'd held her in his arms, kissed her until she was breathless, and yet this innocent gesture was every bit as sensual.

'Anybody for poker?'

Neither of them had heard Broussard reenter the room. Embarrassed, Kacy tugged her hands free and looked over Dan's shoulder to see Big John scratch at his crotch. He stopped when Dan turned around.

'Maybe later,' Dan answered, standing. 'How about refilling the wood box? I'll get the dishes.'

Broussard hadn't struck Kacy as the sort of man who took kindly to being told what to do. She half expected him to tell Dan that she could do the dishes and that he could get his own firewood.

Much to her surprise, he didn't argue.

'Sounds fair,' he answered instead, leaving Kacy and Dan alone again.

By the time Kacy regrouped, Dan had deserted her and stood at the sink. If he thought he could get her off his back that easily, she thought, following him, he was sadly mistaken.

'There's plenty of room on the floor for another pallet,' she went on with the tirade his actions had chased out of her mind earlier. When he ignored her and started running the dishwater, she wanted to slap his hands away from the faucets. Through sheer force of will, she restrained herself.

'Yes . . . ' he began, immersing the stacked dishes in steaming, sudsy water. 'But there are only enough cushions to make one bed and only one sleeping bag. So,' he continued with a devilish grin, 'you have your pick of bunkies. Me or Mr. Prim and Proper.'

Kacy squared her shoulders and fixed him with what she hoped was a piercing glower. 'You and Mr. Emily Post can have the bed. I'll take the floor.'

His fingers wrapped around her arm before she could stalk away. 'That's a solution, but not a good idea.'

She had to do something to stop whatever it was he was doing to her senses — and fast. No man had ever gotten to her the way he did. A threat seemed like a good idea. 'What if I just tell him why I'm here?' she challenged.

What the hell do you think you're doing? was written all over his handsome face, and was exactly what she expected him to say.

But he surprised her. 'What do you think would happen if he got wind of that hundred thousand dollars?' he countered with one raised eyebrow.

So *that* was the reason he had been humoring Broussard all evening. Broussard held the law in contempt and probably didn't believe in the code of honor that supposedly lived among thieves. If he had heard the news reports, he wouldn't think twice about trying to do Dan in to get the money.

Indignation puffed up inside Kacy. 'There wasn't any hundred thousand dollars.'

'You and I are the only ones who know that.'

'Hawkins, you, and I.' She was guessing, of course, but from the expression that flitted across Dan's face, she knew she'd hit a nerve.

He said nothing for several long seconds, reinforcing her conjecture. 'You don't know what you're getting involved in here, Kacy.'

'It doesn't really matter, does it?' she shot back. 'You've seen to it that I'm involved.' She saw the color leave his face and instantly regretted her words. But, as she tried to teach her children at Wee Care, words spoken in anger couldn't be taken back.

He recovered quickly and released her so abruptly that she fell back a step. 'Give this some thought.' This time the challenge was his. 'What made you cozy up to me when we first got back here?'

The answer to that wasn't easy to

explain, not even to herself. At first glance, Broussard had seemed to be her salvation. She remembered hesitating in the beginning only because during the day a part of her had come to trust Dan. But later, standing in front of the fire, watching the byplay between Dan and Broussard, intuition had bid her caution.

'Trust your instincts, Kacy.' Dan closed the gap between them without touching her. 'We'll both have to sleep with one eye open if you're alone on that floor.' He wiped his hands on his shirt front, then tilted her chin up. The way his lips turned up at the corners in that heart-stopper smile of his made it hard for her to think. 'Besides, it's not like we haven't already slept together.'

She wasn't expecting this any more than she'd expected him to kiss her palms. 'It's not the same thing.'

'I know.' His voice was as gentle as his thumb caressing her lower lip. 'And I'm sorry. This isn't the way I want it, either. When we make love, I don't think either of us will want an audience.' He eased her into his embrace so subtly that she didn't realize it until he released her and leaned back to put a little distance between them. 'I promise to be a perfect gentleman.' He kissed her on the tip of her nose. 'Tonight.'

The front door opened to admit Broussard, whose arms were laden with firewood. 'Damn! It's colder'n a witch's — ' His eyes locked with Dan's. 'Well, it's just plain damned cold out there tonight.' He dumped the wood, then brushed himself off before he settled at the bar. 'Where're your cards, Wilder? I feel lucky tonight.'

'Top shelf, in the corner,' Dan said, indicating the bookshelf to the left of the fireplace. 'Just give me a minute to finish up here, and I'll take you on.'

'How 'bout you, little lady?' Broussard asked, fishing his wallet out of his hip pocket and spreading his money out in front of him. 'Care to try your hand at winnin' some of Big John's hard-earned money?'

'I don't know anything about poker.' She found it difficult to meet his cold hazel gaze, but if he called her 'little lady' one more time, she was going to take a very unladylike poke at him.

'Child's play,' Broussard insisted, grabbing the pen with the uninhibited redhead. 'Git me some paper, and I'll jot down the rank of hands for you.'

By the time Kacy found a blank sheet of paper, Dan had finished with the dishes and taken off his boots — and Broussard was enraptured of the redhead. He scribbled on the paper, then shoved it toward Kacy.

'Throat's kinda parched, Wilder,' Broussard said, faking a cough. 'How 'bout 'nother belt of that sissy stuff you call whiskey?'

Dan obliged, then cut the cards.

Broussard began the deal, starting with Kacy, then Dan, and ending with himself. 'You ain't gonna let me drink alone, are you?'

Dan avoided looking at Kacy. 'That wouldn't be very hospitable of me now, would it?' he said, standing and getting himself a glass. 'How about you, Kacy?'

'I'll stick with my soft drink.' She saw in Dan's eyes that was what he wanted her to say. Like it or not, she and her kidnapper had forged an unspoken alliance — them against Big John Broussard.

'Cain't help thinkin' I seen you someplace.'

Broussard was speaking to her, and she glanced up to see his broad forehead wrinkled in a thoughtful scowl. 'You do TV commercials or anything like that?' he asked.

Kacy and Dan exchanged worried glances. 'No,' she replied, her mind awhirl with possible answers. 'But my sister's an actress.' It wasn't exactly a lie. Suzy was a member of the community theater in Dallas. 'We look a lot alike,' she added for good measure. He seemed to accept that, and she saw a wave of relief wash across

Dan's face, which he covered by leaning back and stretching his right leg out so he could empty his pockets. To one side, he laid his keys and loose change; in front of him, he spread out tens and twenties that he took from his billfold.

Each man spotted Kacy twenty dollars, and two hours later, she had paid them each back and was winning big. Broussard's drink had been replenished time and time again, while Dan still nursed his one and only.

'If you gentlemen will excuse me . . .' she said, yawning and pushing back her stool. 'I think I'll say good night. Which side of the bed do you want?' she asked Dan, realizing too late that her question nullified everything they had said and done during the evening to give Broussard the impression that they were lovers. Kacy prayed that he'd had so much to drink that the slip would go unnoticed.

No such luck. His head came up with a jerk.

'Oh, no, you don't,' Dan answered

with a playful shake of his head. 'We're not playing that game tonight.' He faced Broussard with a silly grimace that was intended to elicit sympathy from one man for another. 'Every night it's the same thing. Whichever side I say I want, she does her best to beat me to it.' Green eyes twinkled back at her with mischief. 'Which side do *you* want?'

Broussard blinked his red-rimmed eyes a time or two as if trying to think it out. Then, apparently mollified — or simply giving up — he stood, staggered back a step or two, and announced that he was 'gonna take a leak and hit the sack, too.'

While he was in the bathroom, Kacy eyed Dan appreciatively. 'Smart move.'

'Don't know that I follow you.' His expression of innocence was every bit as counterfeit as it was priceless. He sidestepped her on his way to the den, where he started tossing the sofa cushions to the floor in front of the fireplace.

Kacy followed. 'First, getting him

liquored up so you wouldn't have to worry about him all night. He's had so much to drink that you'll be lucky if you don't have to tuck him in. He'll sleep like a baby tonight.' She dragged out the sleeping bag and pitched it to him. 'And second, for covering my slip-up. You think fast under pressure.'

'I'll take that as a compliment.' Every time he smiled at her, she felt things she had only read about in novels, seen in movies, but had never experienced firsthand. Oh, she knew love — the love of her family, her mother and sisters. And, of course, there was Mandy. But she wasn't exactly sure how she felt or should feel about the unfamiliar emotions Dan Wilder could bring to the surface with just a look or a touch. They were alien and frightening and wonderful — and, considering the circumstances, completely illogical.

By the time Broussard returned, all he had to do was crawl between the covers. In less time than it took to make out the sofa bed, his loud snoring filled the room.

Standing on opposite sides of the bed, Dan and Kacy exchanged a long look. Finally he broke the silence.

'So, which side *do* you want?' He said it jokingly, but neither of them so much as smiled.

Other than the occasional nights that Mandy slipped into bed with her, Kacy had slept alone most of her adult life. She always slept in the middle of the bed. 'This side's okay.'

He nodded, tugging his shirt free from his jeans and beginning to unbutton it. The springs creaked beneath his weight when he sat down on the bed and slipped off his shirt.

Kacy stood rooted to the spot, seemingly spellbound by the sight of the broad shoulders that tapered down to a trim, narrow waist. He leaned forward to remove his socks, and the play of muscles across his back was a symphony of movement. From the back, his biceps were muscular and well-defined, and she remembered the feel of them as he held her in his arms that day. He stood, and suddenly she realized that his jeans were next.

'I'll be right back.'

What a stupid thing to say, she reproached her reflection in the bathroom mirror. Of course she'd be right back. Where else was there for her to go? Stalling for time, she undressed and carefully folded her clothes. Then she took the floral long johns from the peg on the back of the door, stepped into them, and buttoned them up under her chin.

Next, she picked up her toothbrush and frowned at the image staring back at her. *Stop being so skittish. Nothing is going to happen.*

Maybe that was the problem. Maybe she wanted something to happen. And Broussard's presence was stopping her from finding out what it would be like to be with a man of compassion as well as passion.

That's the craziest thought you've

ever had. Only three hours ago hadn't she been on the verge of telling Dan she was having doubts about the unexpected turn in their relationship? *Just be grateful you've been given some time to sleep on it.*

This stupid dialogue with herself was getting her nowhere, so she put her things away and firmly told herself what she told Mandy whenever the child dreaded doing something she had to do: The hard part is getting started; just do it; it won't be as bad as you think. The advice had never failed Mandy and what was good enough for her daughter was certainly good enough for Kacy.

Dan was already in bed by the time she turned out both the bathroom and kitchen lights. She saw him reach over and turn back her side of the covers. He was bare to where the blanket lay folded back at his waist. Suddenly her mouth felt like cotton. Surely he was wearing the thermal bottoms, wouldn't be crass enough to be buck naked . . .

Conscious of every move but determined not to be a ninny about this, she eased in beside him — and immediately rolled toward the sag in the middle of the bed. She came to an unceremonious halt when her body wedged up against his. Stunned, she scrambled for her side only to roll back into the swag.

'It's no use, baby.' Dan's voice was a velvet whisper in the dark. 'The springs are shot. The only way two people can sleep comfortably is if they really like each other.'

Having to sleep in the same bed with him was one thing, but being forced to snuggle was something else altogether. Again she tried to stay on the outer edge of the mattress. As before, she wound up butted snugly against Dan's body.

'You're going to wear yourself out.' His breath fanned her ear, drawing goose bumps on top of goose bumps.

'Fine. I'll wear myself out.' More determined than ever, she groped for the edge one more time.

'What a shameful waste of energy,' he teased, mocking her efforts by reaching for her and easily forcing her into the curve of his body. Backside against him, she struggled with all her might, stopping only when he whispered, 'If you're not careful, you're going to wake *Big* John. And I've known him long enough to know that he'll think we're doing exactly what you're trying so hard to prevent from happening.'

She stopped squirming immediately. What he said had merit. 'All right,' she said through clenched teeth. 'Just let go of me.'

He did as she asked, but let his hand rest intimately on her hip. She tolerated it only because she knew that any ruckus from her would only amuse him.

Broussard turned over on his side and his snoring level dropped a decibel or two. To Kacy's already heightened senses, the sound was still a loud roaring in her ears.

The gentle in and out of Dan's breathing became shallow and even, and, knowing that he was either asleep or close to it, she tried to relax. But the hard length of his body at her back was comforting and warm and, to her mortification, tempting. Try as she might, visions of his bare chest invaded her mind's eye, visions that made her pulse race and her body ache with wanting. *Stop thinking and acting like some lovesick adolescent*, she chided herself. *You're thirty years old, for goodness' sake. Act it.*

The male anatomy was not unfamiliar to her. Physically Ted had been every young woman's ideal — drop-dead gorgeous with the virile body of a youthful athlete. Lovemaking with him, though unfulfilling for her, had never been actually unpleasant, with the exception of those two times —

'I can't do this,' she whispered, doing her best not to make the situation more tense by wiggling away.

'You're not doing anything.'

She repressed the urge to hiss at him like an angry cat. 'You know what I mean.' She sat up. Broussard was a lump of unconsciousness on the floor. 'I can't just crawl into bed with a man I know nothing about.'

Dan rolled over onto his back. 'If it'll help, we can talk for a while. Tell me about yourself and I'll do the same. What do you want to know?'

The fact that he was letting her go first was all that made her agree. Maybe she could steer the conversation away from her when the time came.

'For starters, what's going on between you and Hawkins?'

'It's a long story.'

She thought he was going to clam up on her before they even got started. 'We've got all night with nothing better to do,' she gently encouraged him. 'Besides, isn't it about time you leveled with me?'

He was quiet a long moment before he reached out to gently pull her back to lie alongside him. 'Things aren't what they seem.'

Kacy had already figured that out on

her own. Dan Wilder was no more a bank robber and a kidnapper than she was a female mud wrestler. She scarcely breathed, waiting for him to go on.

'He's responsible for my brother's death.'

Myriad questions filled her mind. How was the banker responsible? What was his relationship with Dan's brother? How did all of this relate to her?

Dan's mood now was tentative, to say the least, and if she wanted to know more, she would have to move slowly.

'You were so angry that first day I saw you in Hawkins' waiting area,' she ventured, wanting to know more, but not wanting to say the wrong thing.

'I'm not proud of my behavior that day,' he admitted. 'I'd just come from Ray's funeral, where I'd had a talk with some cop — FBI agent, actually — who told me enough to link Ray with Hawkins.' The weariness in his voice was more from mental stress than from the long day on the river.

She heard the pain, and although she

wanted to know more, she changed the subject. 'And the money?'

'It was Ray's.' His voice was a grim monotone. 'Actually, it was mine, and I took it back for his family. He left a wife and three boys and more bills than his insurance will cover.'

'And the disks. What did they have to do with all of this?'

'Kacy,' he said with a weary sigh, 'there's enough story here to keep us talking for three days. I promise, I'll tell you all of it one day. It's your turn now.'

This was what she'd been dreading. She *never* talked about Ted.

'Tell me about your family.'

Grateful that he'd chosen a neutral area, she answered honestly. 'My father died when I was a teenager, and my mother remarried a few years later. My stepfather was — ' She wanted to find the right word, but nothing seemed appropriate. 'Well, let's just say he wasn't my father. And I have four younger sisters.'

'A big family. I envy you that.'

'It had its moments.' She smiled to herself, remembering the good times, then turned to him. 'And my sister Suzy really is an actress. In one of the Dallas community theaters.' They both laughed at that.

'Now for the one I know you've been dreading. Tell me about your husband. Ted, wasn't it?'

Kacy felt the warmth leave her body. 'Dan, I really don't — '

He nestled her more closely to him. 'You don't have to tell me anything you don't want,' he said earnestly. 'And I don't want the gory details. I just want to know if he hurt you.'

'No one ever walks away from a divorce unscathed,' she tried to hedge.

'You know that's not what I meant.' His hand began massaging the length of her arm. 'I've known a few battered women, Kacy. I know the signs.'

Kacy wanted anything but Dan Wilder's pity, but she couldn't lie to him. 'He only . . . hurt me on two occasions.' She cleared her throat. 'After the miscarriage, I left him.' It was easier to tell than she'd thought it would be. 'And there's enough story there to keep us talking three more days.' Her laugh was forced and she hoped he would respect her decision to drop the subject there.

Dan gave her a reassuring squeeze. 'Point taken. Tomorrow's going to be a long day for me. Let's get some sleep. We can pick up where we left off when I get back tomorrow afternoon.'

Kacy was satisfied with the little she had learned about Dan, was grateful that he in turn was sensitive to her reluctance to open herself up to the pain. Oddly, though, for the first time in years she didn't feel threatened by her past. Closing her eyes, she tried to fall asleep, but was so acutely aware of his presence that it was impossible.

'Dan?'

His reply was a languid 'Yeah?'

'Just tell me what the Q stands for?'

'Aren't you ever going to give up?'

250

She smiled to herself. 'Guess not. Quincy?'

'No such luck.'

Exasperated, she tried again. 'Quigley?'

He laughed and shook his head. She had come to know him well enough to realize that he was trying to come up with something as silly as Qute.

'Quasimodo. Now go to sleep, baby.' He said it so seriously that she raised her head, sought his face in the semidarkened room. His eyes locked with hers, his gaze drawing her head closer to his until his lips took hers in a kiss so full of tenderness and wanting that it swept away all the hurt and fear that had been a part of her for so long.

And when his hand claimed her breast, it was the most natural, honest thing she had ever experienced. Content, she fell asleep with the sound of his heart beating beneath her ear.

10

'Kacy.' Her name, softly whispered, drifted through her consciousness to ease her from the folds of dreaming. For a change, the dream was pleasant, peaceful, the kind from which she didn't want to wake.

'Kacy,' the voice insisted. 'We're going now.'

She opened her eyes to a room just starting to fill with the first hazy light of the rising sun. Dan's face came into focus, and she raised one hand to caress his whisker-stubbled cheek.

'You didn't shave,' she said through a sleepy smile.

He turned his own smile into her palm before taking her hand in his. 'No time. The sooner we're on the river, the sooner I'll be back. Depending on how long it takes to find Broussard's boat, you'll be alone most of the day.' He pressed something into her hand. 'I can't find my keys, but here's an extra set to the gate and to the gun cabinet.'

Apprehension began to niggle at her. Something was wrong. Fully awake now, she sat up. 'Let me go with you.'

'No,' he said, adamant. 'I'll feel better knowing you're safe here. Lock yourself in once I'm gone. Do you know anything about guns?'

Although it was the last thing she expected him to say, the question didn't shock her. She nodded in answer.

'Handgun or shotgun?'

'Either.' Her father had been an avid sportsman, and had shown all his girls how to handle different weapons.

'Good. The handgun and the twelve-gauge are both loaded and ready. Whichever one you choose, just release the safety, aim, and pull the trigger. There's no way you can miss at close range.' He was preparing her for trouble.

'What you're saying is that I'd be one more thing for you to worry about if I went.' She searched his eyes, knowing they couldn't hide the truth from her. 'You don't trust him, do you?' She saw by his hesitation that he was choosing his words carefully.

'John Broussard's a loner with the morals of a crooked politician. Most people on both sides of the river were glad to see him leave this area three years ago, myself included. The best thing for me to do is help him recover his damned boat and be well rid of him.'

'We're losin' daylight, Wilder,' Broussard called from outside.

Dan glanced toward the door, then back at her. 'Take care of the blisters, and keep the fire going. Another storm and cold front are moving in.' While he spoke, his hands moved up and down the length of her arms. He ran his tongue across his lips, and she could almost taste the kiss they both wanted so badly. 'See you tonight,' he said, hesitating.

If he kissed her, she wasn't sure she

could let him go. As if reading her mind, he brushed his lips across her forehead, then left before either of them said or did something that would make it harder for him to leave.

Outside, she heard the two men talking, planning the excursion down-river. She scrambled from the bed to stand at the window. Broussard was still wearing Dan's clothes, while Dan sported another, heavier coat. The one he'd worn before hung in plain sight on the porch in the morning sun. She watched Broussard take the seat in the front of the canoe and wait for Dan to shove them out into the open water. Once he did, both men started paddling, and, remembering some silly superstition about it being bad luck to watch a loved one until he was out of sight, she turned back to the empty cabin.

A sudden sense of being completely alone and utterly helpless engulfed her. Then, just as suddenly, anger surged within her. *She was not helpless*. She was a survivor, and she would survive this, if for no other reason than that Mandy was waiting for her. And then there was Dan. God, she was confused. What was this . . . attraction growing, burning, between them? Was it genuine or would it disappear when the difficulty they were facing passed? For the first time ever, she let herself think of a father for Mandy. Dan would make a wonderful husband and father.

Enough! she told herself with vehemence. There were other things she could think about, other things she could do. But what? When all else fails, she decided as quickly as she'd asked herself the question, fall back on routine. And the first thing she usually did was eat a hearty breakfast.

A covered dish waited for her on the stove. Kept warm by the heat from the oven, the scrambled eggs, sausage, and biscuits were just what she needed to start the day. Broussard must have made the coffee, because it was bitter-strong. She picked up yesterday's newspaper lying where the ill-bred man had sat last night and began leafing through it while she ate. Yesterday's news was better than another horror novel, she quipped silently — until she came across a photograph of herself on page seven.

Houston Day Care Owner Kidnapped by Bank Robber, the headline above the photo proclaimed in bold letters. With a sinking sensation in the pit of her stomach, she quickly scanned the article. Everything was there: her name, the description of the still-unidentified bank robber, the report that the suspect had made off with one hundred thousand dollars.

The food in her stomach began to churn. Had Broussard seen it? If so, had he made the connection? The photo was a couple of years old. Her hair was shorter, and it wasn't a very good likeness of her as she looked today. But the name, Kacy Angelle, wasn't Jane Smith or Ann Jones or anything else common enough to be confused with another name. What would Broussard do with the knowledge? Was Dan worried that Broussard might try to make it back to the cabin in search of the alleged money? Could that be the reason he'd made such a point of asking her if she could use a gun and told her to lock the gate? Her thoughts took a sudden, more frightening turn. Would the man try to harm Dan while they were alone on the river today? The idea of something happening to him made her blood run cold.

Quickly skirting the bar, she raced across the room and locked the outer gate as Dan had instructed, then dead-bolted the wooden door. Her fingers were trembling when she inserted the other key into the gun cabinet's lock. It turned with ease and she found the two guns he'd mentioned set apart from the others. First she tried the handgun. The feel of it in her hand was alien, but she knew that it would be easier to handle. She placed it on the night table, then took out the twelve-gauge. Huge and heavy, it looked simple enough to use. She found the safety and switched it off and on a few times, getting the feel of the weapon in her hands. She hadn't held a gun since her father's death, but she was confident that she could use either. She leaned the shotgun against the doorjamb and checked for more shells. She smiled at the sight of two boxes, one for each weapon, sitting on the floor of the gun cabinet. Dan had made sure they were where she could see them.

All she had to do now was get dressed and find something to occupy her time for the rest of the day. In the bathroom, she found Broussard's damp clothes slung haphazardly over the shower-curtain rod. His billfold lay in a puddle of water beside the tub. She picked it up and laid it out to dry on the windowsill. Quickly dressing and careful of her blistered hands, she then proceeded to give the bathroom a thorough scrubbing. The nesting instinct had taken control.

After putting the bedding away and folding the hide-a-bed back inside the sofa, she straightened the kitchen until it was spotless, then swept and mopped all the hardwood floors.

The only thing out of place now was the deck of cards still lying on the bar where they'd left them after their poker game last night. Dragging a bar stool with her to the bookshelves, she used it to reach the top shelf, left corner where she knew they were kept.

If she hadn't been standing on the stool, she never would have seen the envelope with Dan's name scrawled across the front of it.

Something told her it was personal, important, and she hesitated to take it down. But something just as strong told her that it held the answers to many of her questions.

With the envelope in hand, she climbed down and curled up in the recliner. The first thing she pulled out was a newspaper clipping. The large black-and-white photo showed the wreckage of a pickup so badly damaged that it was impossible to discern the make and model. A chill spread through her as she read the caption below the mass of twisted metal and broken glass:

'Houston police are investigating the accident that claimed the life of local businessman Raymond Wilder, thirty-two, who is listed in critical condition at St. Joseph Hospital. Witnesses reported observing the vehicle moving erratically through traffic moments before it crossed the median and crashed head-on with an eighteen-wheeler. The truck driver was not seriously injured.

Kacy felt her eyes misting as she pulled several sheets of paper out of the envelope. Unfolding them, she saw at first glance that it was a handwritten letter.

'Dan . . . ' it began. 'Since you're reading this, I will have met with some untimely accident or been openly murdered.

'Before I tell you what I've gotten mixed up in, I have to let you know how much your help and confidence in me have meant all these years. It was never easy being the screw-up in the family, but you were always there to help me fix whatever I'd messed up. It's been hard living in your shadow, being Dan Wilder's younger brother, but you never made me feel inferior, and you never interfered. You let me make my own mistakes, watched me struggle to be as good as you without telling me how to do things. That had to be hard for you, but it was the right thing to do.

'The years I spent with you at Wilder Construction were the cornerstones of my independence. But I wanted to break out on my own too soon. Two years after leaving your company, my own business was slowly going under. I needed a substantial amount of money just to get out of the red. I know you would have loaned me the money, but it was my problem. I couldn't keep running to you for help. I went to bank after bank, one savings and loan after another until I ran across Marcus Hawkins.'

Kacy stopped reading, readjusted herself in the chair. She could feel the tension slowly building within her as she continued. Here Ray told a very familiar story of how Hawkins had turned him down in the beginning because his credit history was insufficient. Later Hawkins called him with the good news that he had 'found a group of investors who make funds available to people unable to acquire backing from conventional sources.' Almost word for word, it was the same spiel he'd given Kacy and Mary after he'd turned down their loan. Marcus Hawkins was a vulture, feeding on the misfortunes of those who came to him in time of trouble. She was no financial wizard, but it took only a few seconds for it all to make sense.

Anger flared inside Kacy as she read

on. 'Looking back now, I see what a fool I was. He insisted that the twenty-five thousand dollars I borrowed from you was merely a show of good faith on my part and would be safe and drawing interest in a certificate of deposit. Hell, Dan, it was his 'finder's fee' from his 'group of investors.' When I realized that I had only five years to make a go of Ray-Lea Construction and pay back the entire loan balance and interest or they could take control of it, I tried to back out. But Hawkins wouldn't budge.

'I couldn't just do nothing, like I usually do. Too much was at stake. I didn't want to get you involved in something that was beginning to stink to high heaven. That's when I went to the law, who put me in touch with Special Agent Hugo Michaelson. With my help, he put together a scheme to end Hawkins's double dealing from his position as loan officer at Southside. We needed proof, and I knew where he kept his records in his office.'

Here the tone of the letter changed. 'I've sent Leanne and the boys to her folks in Colorado where they'll be safe until this is all over, and I pray everything goes like we've planned.

'But this is a rough bunch of people I'm crossing, and, if things go wrong, I'll need you to take care of Leanne for me. You know what a helpless little thing she is. You two could be happy together. And don't let my boys forget me. I'm counting on you, Dan.'

It was signed simply, *Ray*.

Kacy wiped the tears from her cheek and tried to check her temper. Evidently Dan had bailed Ray out of trouble over the years. And now Ray was laying a guilt trip on him from the grave. ' . . . *I'll need you to take care of Leanne . . . you know how helpless she is . . . You two could be happy together . . . Don't let my boys forget me . . .* ' And pairing him off with Leanne in the bargain!

If she hadn't been so engrossed in Ray's letter, she would have heard the faint hum of the outboard motor approaching the cabin. As it was, the greeting called from outside startled her.

'Hello da house,' the male voice rang out.

Half expecting it to be Broussard, she scrambled to crouch below the window. Peeking out, she saw an elderly man helping a slender blonde from the small aluminum boat beached out front. They were talking as they walked, and it took a moment for them to get close enough for Kacy to hear what was being said.

'I don' know 'bout leavin' you here all by youself,' the old man was saying in a thick Cajun accent as they approached. 'I don' see Dan's canoe nowhere.' The man had to be seventy years old if he was a day, and although he walked with the bentover stoop no doubt caused by years of hard work, his gait was quick and sure. Beneath his jacket, badly frayed suspenders held up faded khaki trousers, and the plaid shirt he wore probably had never felt the heat of an iron.

'I'll be okay, Mr. Fontenot,' the woman answered his concern with a voice that was as steady as it was sweet. The crisp December breeze lifted silky strands of long blond hair from her face, and the thing that struck Kacy most was the melancholy she saw in her eyes. 'I'm sure he won't be gone long. See,' she said, pointing toward the cabin, 'smoke's coming out of the chimney, and his coat is hanging there on the porch. He must have gotten caught in one of the storms and left it there to dry.'

They were close enough now that Kacy could see them clearly. The old man's eyes scanned the perimeters, uncertainty creasing his brow. Deeply etched laugh lines at the corners of his eyes and the wrinkles creasing his forehead recorded his yesterdays on his weathered face much like the days of the week mark a calendar. Faded brown eyes told of joys and sorrows past.

Unruly silver-gray hair streaked from beneath the floppy brim of the hat perched atop his head. Two matches, for whatever reason, were stuck inside the hat band, adding a touch more character to his already distinguished appearance.

'Well, all right,' he agreed at last. 'But I'll be back in a couple of hours. I got to check on da Millers. Not ever'one 'long dis ole river's lucky as Dan, him. Lots of dem are havin' ta head for higher ground.' He started to turn away, but stopped. 'Dan's been here off 'n on ever since Ray — ' He dropped his gaze and neither spoke for a second or two. 'I knowed he wanted ta be left alone, so I ain't bothered him none. But, Leanne, I gotta say how sorry I am, me — ' His voice faltered again, and Leanne Wilder reached out and put her hand on his shoulder. 'I've knowed dem two boys since dey was no bigger'n — ' This time he couldn't go on.

'I know, Mr. Fontenot.' Leanne took

the old man's gnarled hand in her own smaller one. 'They think highly of you, too.' They shared a moment of silence that made Kacy feel guilty for spying.

Suddenly Mr. Fontenot said with a shake of his head, 'Jus' look at us. Us almos' done forgot your groceries.' While they returned to his boat, Kacy stood and went to the door. She heard them say their good-byes, and a moment later, Dan's sister-in-law stood staring at her through the barred door.

'I'm sorry if I startled you,' Kacy said, unlocking the gate. 'But Dan said for me to keep the cabin locked.'

'Who are you?' Leanne Wilder wanted to know, her artfully arched eyebrows pulling together above clear blue eyes.

Kacy relieved Leanne of one of the bags. 'My name's Kacy, and I'm . . . here with Dan.' That was as close to the truth as she dared come. From Ray's letter, she assumed that his wife knew nothing about his conspiracy with the law to put Hawkins out of business.

Consequently she probably had no idea that his death was anything but an accident.

'I'm Leanne.' Dan's sister-in-law extended her hand with a smile. 'And I'm glad Dan isn't alone now. Where is he, by the way?'

Both women carried their bags to the kitchen, where they started putting the groceries away. It was apparent that each knew her way around the cabin.

'He had to help John Broussard track down his pirogue. Seems like he overturned it yesterday and was anxious about finding it.'

Leanne's face clouded. 'You mean that man's back?' No sooner were the words spoken than she covered her mouth with the tips of her fingers. 'I'm sorry. That was unkind. But you have to understand, John Broussard doesn't get along with too many people. I think Dan and Ray are the only ones on the river who tolerate him.' What little color there was in her complexion seemed to drain out right there in front of Kacy's eyes. 'I mean, Ray used to tolerate him.' She looked so frail and exhausted that Kacy immediately imagined the countless sleepless nights she'd had since Ray's death.

'You look tired,' she said. 'Have a seat and I'll fix us something to drink. Coffee?'

Leanne smiled her thanks and took a seat at the bar. 'That sounds good.'

Kacy poured them each a cup, then continued to put the groceries away. 'If I knew you better, Leanne, I'd give you a hug.' She looked up to smile at the blonde. 'Fresh vegetables, a roast, honest-to-goodness milk, and not one canned item. I don't mind telling you, I'm about burned out on chili and stew.'

Leanne laughed and Kacy was amazed at the transformation the smile made in her appearance. 'I know what you mean. And isn't that powdered milk the worst?'

Every ounce of tension between them disappeared with the comical grimaces they pulled at each other. 'Have you known Dan long?' Leanne asked over the rim of her mug.

Kacy put her own mug down in front of her. 'Long enough,' she replied. 'I guess you could say he swept me off my feet.'

'That's our Dan.' This time when Leanne laughed, her gaze held Kacy's. 'You're the only woman he's ever brought out here. Not many people know about this camp. It's his closely guarded secret, his getaway, where he comes when the world crowds in on him. You must be someone special.'

If only you knew, Kacy thought, thinking also that Leanne wasn't trying to pump her for information, only that she cared deeply for her brother-in-law. In a matter of minutes, the two women were talking as freely as if they'd been friends for years. After exhausting the topic of the weather, they discussed Mandy and Leanne's three sons, or the Wild Bunch as their uncle Dan called them, then the conversation turned to what was dearest to Leanne's heart.

'Did you know Ray?' she asked, going on when Kacy shook her head in answer. 'I remember the day I met him.' Her blue eyes glazed over with the memory. 'It was shortly after Ellie's death.' She stopped and looked at Kacy.

'He told me about his wife,' Kacy assured Leanne, who looked relieved that she hadn't said something out of line.

'Dan has a cabin not too far from my family's horse ranch in Colorado that makes this one look like the Embassy Suite at the Diplomat. Talk about rustic. Anyway, Ray had come there with Dan because he didn't want him being alone so soon after Ellie's funeral, and we met at a little cafe where I was a waitress.' She raised her gaze to meet Kacy's. 'Do you believe in love at first sight?'

Had Kacy been asked that question a month ago, she probably would have answered no. Now, she realized, she'd loved Dan from the moment she'd seen him in Hawkins's waiting area. Of course, she hadn't recognized it until now because so many other emotions — fear, confusion, anger — had camouflaged it.

'Yes, Leanne. I believe a woman recognizes her soul mate the instant she sees him.' And it was true. Dan Wilder was her soul mate, her love, mysterious Q and all.

A tear trickled down Leanne's cheek. 'Nine days after we met, we were married, and I finally met Dan.' She wiped the tears away and laughed. 'What a meeting that was. Dan and I didn't like each other from the word go. Looking back now I see why. Ray had shared Dan with Ellie for years, but Dan had never had to share his brother with anyone. And I was a new bride who wanted Ray all to myself. It was a rough year for all of us. I remember the day we finally accepted each other. I had the most wonderful news, but instead of waiting to share it with Ray when we were alone, I sat them both down in my living room and told them that we were having a baby.' Her face came alive with the memory. 'You should have seen them. Ray just sat there like he was in shock while Dan swooped me up and whirled me around the room.'

Kacy felt the sting of tears in her eyes as Leanne went on. 'It was like that with each baby. Dan was always so happy for Ray and was with him at each birth. I think he loves Ray's children so much because he has none of his own. Ellie wasn't able to have children.'

Kacy had forgotten that Dan had told her that, and she felt an unexpected pang of anxiety. Long ago she had come to grips with the fact that she would never bear children of her own. Would that make a difference to Dan? If the time ever came, could he accept Mandy as his daughter?

'Kacy,' Leanne interrupted her thoughts. 'I'm pregnant again. Ray didn't know — '

The sound of heavy steps on the

porch cut off Leanne's words. The door opened and Dan came walking in.

'I thought I told you to keep the gate locked,' he said before he saw Leanne, who was off the stool and in his arms before he could say another word.

'I think I'll get the roast in the oven,' Kacy said, excusing herself and leaving the two with as much privacy as close quarters allowed.

Dan led Leanne to the sofa. 'I thought you were in Colorado with the boys,' Kacy heard him say.

'I was. But when I couldn't get you at the office or your house, I had to come back and make sure you were okay. I knew you'd be here.' Leanne's voice was shaky. 'When I saw that the roads were flooded, I went to Mr. Fontenot. He'll be back to pick me up later.'

'Then your folks are taking care of the Wild Bunch.'

'Yes. They're having the time of their lives. Dad's teaching them to ride.'

The room grew quiet after that, and Kacy glanced up from scrubbing carrots to see Dan still holding Leanne in the protective circle of his arms. She also saw the clipping of the wreck and Ray's letter where she'd left them on the table next to the recliner. There was no way for her to get them out of sight without drawing attention. She could only hope that Leanne wouldn't see them.

'You have to go back today,' Dan shocked them both by saying abruptly.

Leanne's head came up off his shoulder. 'I don't understand.'

Dan stood and removed his coat and hat. 'I know you don't, but do it anyway.' Kacy had never heard him speak so sternly before and wanted to come to Leanne's aid at once. She needn't have worried, because Leanne was on her feet and glaring up at him in an instant.

'Don't give me orders, Dan.' She faced him with determination in her stance. 'I put up with Ray's chauvinistic pampering because I loved him, but I won't take it from you.' A tigress came

277

to life right before their eyes. 'I'm not as helpless as he wanted me to be.'

Dan glowered down at her. 'What's that supposed to mean?'

Kacy expected Leanne to back down under Dan's penetrating gaze, but she didn't.

'Dan . . . ' she began, her voice softening, but steady. 'We both know how inferior Ray always felt compared to you. He was my hero, just like you were his. With me he was the man he wanted to be, not Dan Wilder's little brother.'

Kacy cast a guilty glance at Ray's letter lying not ten feet away. Ray's words coming out of his widow's mouth were eerie.

'And don't look so guilty,' she went on, reaching up to caress his cheek. 'You couldn't be less a man just to make your brother look good. He knew that. I loved him without question, and I guess I'm as guilty as he was for the way he treated me, like I was some sort of helpless creature that needed protecting all the time. And now you're picking up where he left off. You're hiding something from me, just like he was when he insisted that I take the boys to Colorado.' Her bravado had picked up as she spoke and Kacy could see that she was determined to know the truth. 'Who is Hawkins and what was Ray doing talking with the FBI?'

She also could see the struggle going on within Dan. He wanted to protect Leanne and preserve his brother's memory as well. No matter his good intentions, Ray Wilder had recklessly put his life on the line trying to save face.

'Everything you just said is true . . . ' he began. 'But now's not the time, Leanne. It's dangerous to be around me right now, and you have three little ones to think about. Things should be settled in a few months, then I'll tell you everything. I promise.'

Again Leanne moved into his embrace, and this time Kacy could only guess at the muffled words she said into his shirt. Dan looked relieved, then he saw the letter lying out in the open. He shot a look across the room at Kacy. Taking advantage of the moment, she discreetly retrieved the letter and put it away.

'There's one other thing,' he said, holding Leanne at arm's length, then releasing her. 'I've put some money in an account for you.' He opened the trunk closest to the door and took out the passbook Kacy had seen the day before. 'I know everything's tied up right now, and — '

Leanne looked at the account book like it was a vile thing. 'I can't take your money, Dan.'

Dan's shoulders straightened visibly. 'Believe me, I hear what you're saying, but it's not my money, honey. I want to buy Ray-Lea from you as soon as we can move on it. I don't want a bunch of strangers taking control of Ray's business. Can you look at it as an advance on the sale? It would sure help me rest easier knowing that you're taken care of.'

Leanne nodded wordlessly, and Kacy was as relieved as Dan. They settled back on the sofa and she heard them discussing the signature card, the sale of Leanne's house, the insurance settlement, and the creditors who were already breathing down Leanne's neck. In the background she also heard something else.

'Dan,' Kacy interrupted. 'I think I hear Mr. Fontenot coming back. I'll wait outside for Leanne while you two finish up in here.' She took down his coat and went outside. Watching Mr. Fontenot ease into shore, she raised a hand and waved.

'Leanne will be right out,' she called, smiling. He waved back and waited patiently in the boat. If she wanted to leave, now was her chance. Dan couldn't stop her without raising a lot of questions Kacy knew he wouldn't want to answer. But did she want to leave? And if she did, what would it mean as far as Dan's safety was concerned?

Moments later as she walked with Leanne toward the waiting boat, she asked, 'You didn't tell him about the baby, did you?'

'No.' It was a simple enough answer, but Leanne searched Kacy's face for the briefest moment. 'I know Dan better than he thinks. If I tell him I'm pregnant, he'll just feel obligated to follow me to Colorado to make sure I'm all right. I want him to be happy, and I sense something special between you two.'

She gave Kacy a hug and joined Mr. Fontenot in his flat-bottomed boat. It took every ounce of strength Kacy possessed to keep from asking Leanne to go see Mary and Mandy and explain that she was fine, that she was in no danger. But that would undoubtedly lead to questions, and until she knew that Dan was going to be safe, she couldn't take a chance on letting anyone know where she was — not even her daughter.

Watching them disappear around the first bend in the river, she felt Dan standing behind her.

'You could have gone with them,' he said. 'I couldn't have stopped you.'

'I know.'

He was so close that she could feel the warmth of his body next to hers. 'What I told her about it being dangerous to be with me was true.' His words rustled near her ear.

Kacy couldn't help herself. She leaned against the muscular length of him, gave herself over to the sense of security she felt just being near him. 'I know that, too.'

'Then why did you stay?'

'I don't know.'

His arms wrapped around her, pulled her so close that she could feel the trembling of his great body as he whispered, 'I think you do.'

11

The instant Kacy stepped out of Dan's arms and went inside, he knew she needed time alone to think about what she'd just done — chosen to stay with him instead of going home to her little girl. The only reason he could fathom was that she'd read Ray's letter and realized just how much danger they'd all be in if she went home now.

Part of him couldn't believe that she had stayed. Another part was happier than he could remember being in a long, time. And yet another part was angry with himself for not insisting that she go with Leanne, quietly get Mandy, and take an extended vacation until this was all over. He was confident that no one could track them here. Over the years, he and Ray had zealously guarded the camp's location, and only Percival Fontenot knew of their life in

Houston. Still, Dan wasn't about to underestimate his adversaries. They, like the law, had their ways of tracking people down.

And, thinking of the law, Michaelson should have received the disks yesterday and by now knew who had sent them. Not that it mattered, but Dan had no way of knowing how long it would take Michaelson's people to gain access to the information stored on the floppies. Depending on how imaginative Hawkins had been in selecting a password for his files, it could take as little as a few minutes or as long as days to retrieve his records.

From the moment he saw Ray's letter out in the open, Dan knew Kacy wouldn't tell anyone who he was or where he'd held her captive for four days. She was bright enough to figure out what was going on, but was sure to have a head full of questions for him. As she'd said last night, it was time he leveled with her.

He slapped his hat against his thigh

and glanced toward the cabin. A little more time, he thought, cursing himself for a coward as he trudged past the front steps and around back, then he would face her.

* * *

Kacy checked the roast again and decided that it was time to add the carrots, onions, and potatoes. Adding seasonings to the bowl of raw vegetables she'd prepared earlier, she arranged them around the roast in the cast-iron Dutch oven and returned it to the oven. She could hardly wait to eat a meal that hadn't been scraped out of a can.

Glancing up, she saw Dan standing just outside the kitchen window. His eyes were trained toward the back of the wooded lot, but she saw nothing out of the ordinary. His stance was wary, his face serious. Had he sensed danger of some sort? Her eyes automatically sought the handgun still lying on the table in the den, then the shotgun next to the door.

Before she could react, she saw him ease toward a small shed nestled among the pine trees lining the far left side of the backyard. Slowly, as if calculating each movement, he opened the door, then disappeared inside. Seconds later he came out. In one hand she saw a bag of something she couldn't quite make out, in the other, a pair of leather work gloves. Tucking the bag under one arm, he pulled on the gloves, then hunkered down low to the ground. Carefully he reached into the bag, withdrew a handful of whatever was inside, then tossed it as far as possible in front of him.

A rustle from the edge of the woods that surrounded the cabin caught Kacy's attention. She glanced that way to see a squirrel try to scamper toward the feed scattered between it and Dan. Suddenly the furry creature lunged awkwardly only to fall to its side, fight to right itself, then try again. What,

Kacy wondered, was wrong with it? While the animal struggled, Dan stood to a low crouch and moved forward, closing the gap between him and the injured squirrel. He hunkered down again, this time holding out the food in his gloved hand. Fascinated, Kacy watched the drama unfold before her, saw the squirrel that she now could see was wet and muddy hesitate and try to scurry away. Again it floundered, but this time Dan got to it before it could right itself.

She couldn't hear his words but knew that he was speaking to the creature in soft, soothing tones as he worked to free it from the plastic six-pack ring that was wrapped around its tiny body. Somehow the animal had become so badly entangled that it was impossible for it to do anything to protect itself. With more patience than Kacy had ever witnessed, Dan worked around tiny sharp teeth and angry claws until he was forced to sit down. Holding the squirrel firmly in one hand, he stretched out his right leg and dug into his pocket. Because of the gloves and the frightened squirrel's frantic squirming, it took some doing, but he was finally able to open his pocket knife. In a matter of seconds, the squirrel was free to scurry up a mammoth live oak tree. There, safely out of reach on a sprawling branch, it stopped to chatter down noisily at Dan. She heard him laugh at the rancorous scolding, then saw him take the bag and pour piles of feed out in several locations before putting it back in the shed.

There wasn't a doubt in her mind now that she'd done the right thing. No man that tender and caring could purposely hurt another human being.

Almost as if her thoughts had reached out and tapped him on the shoulder, Dan raised his head and looked at her. They exchanged a look that spoke volumes before he broke the eye contact to walk around the side of the cabin. A moment later, he entered the front door.

Kacy needed to be the one to initiate the conversation. 'You could have been hurt,' she said with the bite of an anxious mother, noting that his shirt was as muddy as it was wet.

Dan shook off the reprimand like an incorrigible child. 'I had it under control. Bullwinkle doesn't behave like that normally.'

'Bullwinkle?' Kacy wondered if she looked as incredulous as she sounded. 'You *named* a wild animal?'

'Actually, he's not as wild as he seems, and several of them have names,' he explained, plucking the wet shirt away from his skin and tugging it free of his jeans. 'When I'm here, I set out feed for whatever comes close enough to the cabin. Bullwinkle usually comes right up to me, but today he was scared. He'd have gnawed his way free eventually, but I didn't want him injuring himself.' He was in the process of unbuttoning his shirt when he sniffed the air and grinned. 'Smells good. How long till supper?'

Kacy didn't see any sense in putting off the inevitable. 'Long enough for us to talk.' She made herself maintain her air of equanimity. She'd made her decision this afternoon and now it was time to see if it had been the right one.

'You're calling the shots.' He gestured toward the sofa. 'We might as well be comfortable.'

Her idea of comfortable was the recliner. His, after she refused the sofa, was the hearth. They faced each other with solemn faces.

'I take it you read Ray's letter.' Dan broke the silence without accusation.

'Yes.'

'Where do you want to start?'

Kacy gathered her thoughts. 'Let's see how much of this I have figured out.'

Dan leaned forward to rest his forearms across his knees and laced his fingers together. 'Agreed.'

'Marcus Hawkins is running an illegal loan operation from his position at Southside, probably fronting for a local crime syndicate.' She waited for him to affirm this much. He nodded and she went on. 'Whenever someone comes to him for money and doesn't qualify for a legitimate loan, he sends him on his way, then contacts him later with an offer he can't refuse.' She hadn't meant to make such an obvious reference to the infamous line from *The Godfather,* and gave him a humorless smile in apology. 'Ray fell for it, then tried to back out. When Hawkins wouldn't let him, Ray went to the law, but they were unable to protect him after Hawkins found him out.' She paused before adding, 'And you're trying to finish the job that killed your brother.'

A wan smile flitted across Dan's somber features. 'You're pretty good at this.'

'Only because Mary and I fell victim to Hawkins's scheme, too. But it took us five years to have it hit us in the face.' She lowered her lashes and when she spoke again, even she heard the self-reproach in her voice. 'I don't know how I could have missed that clause about the balloon payment when we signed the contract.'

'Don't be so hard on yourself,' Dan was quick to console. 'Hawkins is a pro. Did he give you a copy of the contract that day or did he mail it to you later?'

Kacy thought back. 'Now that you mention it, he said that he had to have another loan officer sign it, too, and that he was out with the flu. He promised to mail the signed contract to us as soon as possible, which he did. What difference does that make?'

'Once you'd signed the contract, it wouldn't have been any problem to add a page to the original copy, one that outlined the payment schedule and the balloon payment with the lender's right to waive negotiation.'

'How could we have been so stupid?'

'With two floppy disks of records, it doesn't look like you were the only ones.' Dan was giving all the support he could from the distance that separated them. 'From all outward appearances, the whole thing looks legitimate enough. And I can understand how someone who'd been turned down time and time again would be more than willing to pay a little extra interest to get the money he needed.'

Kacy, knowing he was really talking about his brother, merely nodded. 'I see what you're saying, and I can understand how taking over a business with assets like heavy equipment and development contracts could be profitable. But how in the world would an operation like Wee Care be of value to people like that?'

'After Ray's death, I did a little investigating on my own. I remember seeing somewhere that Hawkins's wife owns a chain of day-care centers in Harris County.' Kacy wanted to reach out and smooth his forehead when it wrinkled in thought. 'What was the name . . . ?'

'Bright and Early Play Schools?'

Dan snapped his fingers. 'That's it.'

Kacy felt a tightening in her solar plexus. 'Regina Hawkins is every independent child care operator's biggest competitor in the Houston area. Why didn't I make the connection before?' she asked glumly. 'If we don't stop Hawkins before the fifteenth of December, Wee Care will become another Bright and Early.'

Dan didn't respond. 'Looks like our boy went out on his own on this one,' he muttered, more to himself than to Kacy. 'He's probably in more trouble than he knows.' Suddenly his head came up. 'What?' His dark eyebrows pulled together, creating several grooves above his green eyes. 'We aren't doing anything. *I'll* take care of Hawkins.'

Kacy didn't like his tone. 'Look,' she said, coming to her feet, 'I have more than a business to lose here. If Wee Care goes belly up, I could lose Mandy. Besides, I can help.'

'No.' He didn't have to raise his voice as he stood to tower over her. That his mind was set was evident in every aspect of his demeanor, from the determined thrust of his jaw to the immutability of his stance. 'I've gone this far on my own. There's no sense putting anyone else in danger.'

Arguing with him at this point was useless. Maybe reasoning would work. 'Dan, let's talk sensibly. Two plans are better than one. You've got Hawkins's records, but what if something goes wrong? I'm already involved. I have my loan papers right here in my purse. That's why I was at the bank both times you were. And I'm willing to help you fight this thing.'

'Absolutely not.' If she thought he'd been tough on Leanne earlier, it was nothing compared to now. 'I'd better clean up before we eat.' Obviously, as far as he was concerned, the conversation was over.

★   ★   ★

The roast was so tender that it fell apart with the touch of a fork. The carrots and potatoes were perfect, the salad crisp and fresh. It was the first real meal Dan had enjoyed in weeks.

He glanced across the bar at Kacy and still couldn't believe that she had stayed. More to the point, that he had *let* her stay. Suddenly, and with startling clarity, he realized why. Kacy Angelle filled an empty spot in his life, an emptiness he had stubbornly refused to acknowledge all these years. Since Ellie's death, he had been more than content to live his life vicariously through Ray's family. That wasn't healthy, he knew, looking back, but Ellie had been the best part of his life and he couldn't imagine anyone else taking her place.

Until now. And, he acknowledged with unshakable conviction, Kacy hadn't taken Ellie's place. In just four short days, she had unobtrusively created her own place in his heart with nothing more than her unwavering courage and her growing trust in him. She was like no woman he had ever known, and for that he was truly thankful.

'Dan?'

He was still looking at her, but he hadn't a clue as to what she had said to him.

'Are you okay?'

Her worried expression made him feel guilty. He reached across the table and laid his hand on top of hers. 'Yeah.' He couldn't help smiling. 'I've never been better.' She looked uncomfortable, so he released her hand. 'Great meal,' he said, noticing that she had hardly touched the portions on her own plate.

Her only response was a polite smile.

'Are you okay?'

She raised her dark-brown eyes, and he knew exactly what was going on behind them. She was scared. Not of him, of that he was certain, but of the memories of her ex-husband that intimacy might bring out of hiding.

'Nothing's going to happen between us, Kacy, unless it's what you want.' He had never seen color flush a face so fast, and again he smiled. 'You did the cooking tonight. I do the cleaning.'

'I like the way you delegate duties, but I don't mind helping,' she offered, standing.

'No deal.' He took her plate and gave her a gentle shove toward the bathroom. 'I think a nice long soak in a tub of hot water is just what you need to relax. And,' he said with one raised eyebrow, 'I won't take no for an answer. At least not about this.'

★   ★   ★

Dan was standing with one foot resting on the hearth when Kacy came out of the bathroom half an hour later. The soak in the tub was, indeed, just what she had needed. She'd had time for soul searching. And out of it all one thing stood out above all else: Dan Wilder was everything she could ever want in a man.

Somewhere in the distance, thunder rumbled, a long and sorrowful peal that echoed its lonely cry through the night. She knew the instant he was aware of her presence in the room. The blood coursing through her veins seemed to thunder in her ears as he straightened and turned his eyes on her. Wearing nothing but his chambray work shirt, she was surprised that his gaze didn't follow the long length of her legs and up. Instead, his clear green eyes locked with hers, and she saw in them his need for reassurance.

Without a word, she went to the sofa and began to remove the cushions. Tonight they would not lie on the floor in front of the fire. One by one, she stacked them on top of each other in the corner closest to the sofa bed, then she faced Dan.

His shirt had been pulled from the waistband of his jeans and lay open to reveal the solid wall of his chest, the flat contours of his stomach. The man exuded sexuality, mystery, and danger. Music played softly in the background, a country ballad she recognized.

They met in the middle of the room without touching.

'We haven't had much of a court-ship,' Dan said, his voice thrilling her with its husky quality. He held out his hand, and she stepped into the circle of his waiting arms. Together, in a rustic log cabin, in the middle of a Louisiana river bottom, with the law and the mob looking for them, they waltzed around the firelight-bathed room. Nestled against the lean, muscular length of him, Kacy turned her face into the hollow of his neck. The fragrance of his cologne mingled with the smells of soap and toothpaste and the scent that was uniquely his, and she lost her battle for control. Her lips brushed his skin and she heard him moan.

They stopped dancing as the lyrics and music continued. Dan's arms tightened around her, then relaxed. Kacy raised her face to his, waited for his lips to descend on hers, and knew that if he didn't kiss her soon she would take matters into her own hands. She trembled with expectation, knew that he'd felt it, too, when he stepped away.

Concern etched his rugged features. 'Are you afraid?'

'Of you?' she asked with a throaty laugh.

He was more serious than she had ever seen him. 'Of us. Of what we've become to each other?' She should have known to expect nothing less than honesty from Dan Wilder. No wonder she loved him.

She loved him.

'I feel a lot of things about us,' she said with such sincerity that she felt the sting of tears in her eyes. 'But scared isn't one of them.' She couldn't wait a moment longer. She reached up, her fingers sliding through the thickness of his dark hair, and drew his head down to hers. The kiss she initiated was tentative in the beginning, a testing of feelings. Then it intensified. His lips parted at the gentle insistence of her tongue, and she was awash in sensations she had never known. Her free

302

hand slipped inside his shirt to explore the marvelous mass of skin and muscle that was Dan. His hands were not idle, either; freely they roamed the curves and contours of her back to cup her buttocks, press her against the evidence of his desire for her.

Suddenly he broke away. 'God, what am I doing?' He said it with such passion that she had to blink back her confusion. 'You deserve so much more. Life has dealt you more than your share of heartache. Your future should be filled with the promise of rainbows and love songs. Right now all I have to offer is the prospect of uncertainty.' He laughed, and the self-mocking sound tore at Kacy's heart. 'Dammit, would you listen to me. I sound more like a poet with noble intentions than a Texas renegade.'

Gently, lovingly, she caressed his cheek. 'Tonight we have firelight and a love song and a sorry excuse for a bed.' A tear escaped to roll down her cheek. 'And each other.'

An obvious wave of relief washed over his chiseled features. 'Speaking of that sorry excuse for a bed . . . ' he said after a moment of reflection. 'We'd better do something about it.' In a matter of seconds, the bed was folded out and their clothes lay in a discarded heap on the floor. This time when they came together, Kacy knew there would be no turning back.

Until he whispered, 'Are you protected, baby?'

In her urgency to convince him of her love, she had forgotten that she hadn't told him that she could never bear children. She couldn't let this go on until he knew that she was barren.

'If you're talking about pregnancy . . . ' She studied his face above her own and felt a sudden sense of loss. What if he couldn't accept it? What if he wanted children of his own to carry on the Wilder name? 'I've only carried one baby.' She dropped her gaze to the mat of curly hair covering his chest. 'After the miscarriage I was told that I could never conceive — '

He silenced her with a kiss that made all the others between them pale by comparison. 'It doesn't matter.' And she saw in his eyes that he spoke the truth.

She smiled up at him. 'And if you mean the other, I haven't — ' Mary often teased her about her celibate lifestyle, but this was embarrassing. 'I mean — '

'Well, I have, and it's okay,' he said, kissing her on the tip of her nose. 'I have it covered.' They stared at each other blankly, then simultaneously broke into laughter.

When he rolled her onto her back and under him, Kacy felt an unexpected pang of panic. The weight of his body brought back a flash of unpleasant memories, and she couldn't control the shudder that passed through her.

As if sensing what had happened, Dan levered his body off hers. Then he waited.

She felt the swollen hardness of him

pressing against her stomach, knew a moment of hesitation before she let her fingers wander through the hair on his chest that tapered downward, pointing the way to his manhood. Once there, she felt her power over him when he breathed her name into the night. With a boldness she didn't realize she possessed, she gave him a gentle shove, rolled with him as he lay on his back. Straddling him, she looked down into eyes darkened with restrained passion and she was touched by the control she knew he was exercising.

She loved the feel of him, the beauty of him. 'You are beautifully put together, Daniel Q. Wilder,' she whispered, trailing kisses from his navel to the pulse at the base of his throat.

His hands covered her breasts, gently kneading them as he eased her back and returned her gaze. 'And you're more beautiful than I'd imagined.' Now his hands moved to the gentle curve of her waist, down to her hips, then between their bodies, where he gently guided himself inside her. His touch was electrifying and her senses came to life like so many live wires. Never had she felt so complete, filled with such joy that tears threatened to overcome her. But it wasn't only the growing ache that cried out from the very core of her that urged her on; it was also an undeniable and boundless emotional need to become one with the man she loved.

Together they began to move in the universal dance of male and female, slowly at first, building the rhythm and the tension to the pinnacle of their passion. She cried out his name as the painful, wondrous, exquisite tightening in her loins suddenly broke for the first time in her life and poured from her. She heard her own name repeated over and over, felt Dan start moving again beneath her. Leaning down to kiss him, her breasts brushed his chest, their swollen and budding tips acting as conductors for sensations so new to her, and that something wonderful happened again. Dan held her tightly, absorbing the aftershocks of her climax with his own.

When at last they both lay spent and content, Kacy felt him ease her off him to lie alongside his perspiration-soaked body. She drew one knee up and over him, leaving her body half covering his. His hands roved up and down her back, caressing, loving, massaging. She felt loved and satisfied and revered — and she never wanted the feeling to stop.

Giddy, she laughed against his chest and hugged him with all her might.

'Feels good, doesn't it?' she heard him say.

'Oh, yes,' she answered, praying that they were talking about the same thing.

'I didn't know I missed being loved so much.' His hands stopped. 'Or loving.'

She hadn't dared say it out loud, and now that he had, the tears started to fall. They wouldn't stop. He didn't try to console her with words, he just held her until it was all out, then he tilted her head back and kissed her until the tears were but a memory. *This* was what love was all about. Knowing and caring what the other was feeling.

'All better?'

She nodded, reveling in the feel of chest hair on her cheek. Suddenly her stomach rumbled, loud and long.

His chuckle was the most wonderful sound she could remember ever hearing. 'I think I'll take that as a yes and a compliment. I covered your plate and left it on the stove. Want some company?'

'Wouldn't have it any other way.' She sat up and started to get out of bed.

He stopped her with one hand. 'Would you do something for me?'

She saw the remnants of passion lurking in his eyes. 'Oh, no. Tell me you're not getting kinky on me,' she teased, knowing she'd do anything he asked of her.

He leaned back and took something from the night table. Dangling from his fingers she saw her black lacy bra and panties. 'I've ached to see you in these from the first time I saw them hanging in the bathroom.'

Her mouth dropped open. 'I'm lying here in your bed naked as the day I was born and you're asking me to *put clothes on*.' Quickly giving him a kiss she knew would make him want her to stay exactly where she was, she broke away and snatched the underwear from him. 'Kinky,' she repeated with an impish grin and rolled out of the bed.

Kacy had never considered herself particularly sexy or desirable until she saw it reflected in Dan's eyes as he watched her step into the panties. She pulled them up, slowly adjusted the high French-cut leg openings and preened from side to side for him. The bra was next, and to her delight, his reaction to her little floor show was evident under the sheet.

'Absolutely perfect.' His expression was as serious as his voice.

Before he could stop her, she grabbed the chambray shirt and drew it on. She didn't, however, button it. She might be modest, but she wasn't stupid.

'Now,' she said, eyeing him appreciatively. 'What do I want you to wear?' Quickly scooping up all his clothes, she skirted the foot of the bed to put the recliner between them.

Calling her bluff, Dan grinned and stood up. There wasn't a modest bone in his body. 'I can take anything you care to dish out,' he said without an ounce of timidity.

Her dark eyes took in every inch of him and she immediately felt her body flushing with desire. For her own peace of mind, she would have to back down.

'Here,' she said, tossing him his jeans. 'I'm hungry and you're distracting.'

He caught the jeans in midair with one hand. 'I'm beginning to get a little hungry myself.' The sexual innuendo thrilled her, but she was getting lightheaded from not eating. She dropped the rest of his clothes in the chair and gave him a look that made him grimace in disappointment. She watched him step into his jeans and button them up, marveling again at the love she had found in such an unlikely place.

While she ate, they talked foolishness, like a couple of teenagers, laughed incessantly, and touched at every opportunity. Standing at the sink later, Kacy felt Dan behind her. He lifted her hair off her shoulder to brush his lips against her neck. A shiver of desire swept over her as his arms came around her, stunning her with its intensity. His fingers splayed across her bare stomach, and again she felt the pressure of his maleness, this time pressing against her backside. Wantonly she rubbed against him and basked in the sound of his throaty moan when he turned her roughly into his embrace.

'Just wanted you to know that I'd go to any lengths to please you,' he said, the words falling on her lips. It was her turn to moan softly, accept the insistent probing of his tongue. In less time than it took to rid themselves of their clothes, they were back in that sorry excuse for a bed.

Dimly Kacy was aware that the rain had returned. This time the thunder and lightning were more forceful than before. But that wasn't what distracted her. She stiffened and Dan immediately sensed that something was wrong.

'I feel like someone's watching me,' she whispered, her eyes scanning the firelit room.

Dan raised up, his green gaze impaling her dark ones. 'I haven't taken my eyes off you all evening.'

This time when they came together, the only thing stronger than the storm raging outside was the intensity of their loving.

12

The first light of day filtered through the window, reaffirming what Kacy had accepted during the wee hours of morning — since last night, her life had started anew. She rested on her side, content to lie there quietly and watch the gentle rise and fall of Dan's chest while he slept. Even in sleep, the raw masculinity of him struck her. His raven hair, streaked at the temples with silver, begged for her attention, and she obliged by lightly running her fingers through its thickness. Long dark lashes fluttered against his sun-browned cheeks. She could look at his face forever — and his body wasn't bad, either.

Firm and perfectly toned, it would be the envy of any man as many as ten years his junior. His arms were muscular, though not overly so, his chest broad and well developed and covered with a crisply curling mat of dark hair. Shamelessly she let her gaze follow the trail of hair that tapered downward until it disappeared beneath the sheet.

More daring than she thought she could ever be, she let her fingers make bold, circular motions around his navel — and lower.

His abdomen tightened, and the smile that tugged at the corners of her lips broadened when he said in a sleepy drawl, 'Keep that up, baby, and you'll have your hands full.'

She raised her gaze to see his lips turned up in a crooked little half-smile. He lifted her hand and kissed her knuckles, then turned it over and brushed his lips across the blisters that were healing nicely.

'Promises, promises,' she couldn't resist taunting back, loving the sleepy, husky quality of his voice.

Moving more quickly than anyone who had just awakened should be able to, he flipped her to her back and she was the one being scrutinized.

'My turn,' he drawled with the lazy smile that did crazy things to her thought processes. Braced on one elbow, he brought his free hand up to cup one breast, explored its peak by circling it with his thumb until the dusky tip grew taut and ached for the gentle suction of his lips. He read her body's signals with uncanny exactness; his mouth covered the rosy peak, his tongue and gentle suckling drawing sounds of delight from her. When she thought she could stand it no longer, his teeth gently nipped and she was sure that she would die from wanting him. His hand migrated lower, his fingers slipping intimately between her thighs to gently massage, then stroke in and out, ultimately bringing her closer and closer to the brink of satisfaction she had experienced time and time again during the night. She wanted to give him the same pleasure, but he covered her body with his, using his knees to spread her legs for him.

Their bodies came together as naturally as breathing. Once again she felt herself drowning in her feelings for him. She tried to get closer, her mind and body recognizing him as her perfect lover. His murmured words of love and sex urged her onward, upward to yet unexperienced heights of ecstasy, and then they were clinging to each other as they drifted back down.

Moments later, Kacy opened her eyes to see him revering her with an expression she had never seen before — one of absolute adoration.

'Just think, if Miss Ross hadn't walked in and thought I was robbing Hawkins, you and I never would have happened,' he said so seriously that she wanted to hold him again. But suddenly he was someplace else, and she didn't have the heart to bring him back before he had it out of his system. Besides, when they weren't making love or sleeping during the night, he'd quietly listened as she exorcised her painful past — the death of her beloved father, her alcoholic stepfather, Ted's obsessions and abuse, and the loss of her baby. Now it was his turn.

'All I wanted was to get Hawkins' records, turn them over to Michaelson, and then keep out of sight until Hawkins and the syndicate bosses were taken into custody. But Miss Ross came in, and when she didn't recognize me, I thought my plan would still work. I knew Hawkins wouldn't identify me and that he would have no choice but to go along with her account of the holdup.

'Then, there you were. You could tell them that I was the same man who had barged into Hawkins' office before. Miss Ross would know exactly who you were talking about, leaving me no choice but to bring you with me. I knew that Hawkins' people would be watching Michaelson, and I wasn't taking any chances that he could protect you. I'd put you in danger by association. The only thing I could do was get you out of

Houston until I could find another way of getting the disks to Michaelson.' As if he suddenly realized his digression, he smiled weakly. 'And then we happened. The one good thing to come out of all of this. Did I remember to tell you that I love you?'

'In every way but words.'

'I love you, Kacy Angelle.' His impassioned words were as demonstrative as his kiss. 'I love everything about you, from that adorable cleft in your chin and the way you kick the cover off your feet in your sleep, to the way you keep bugging me about my mid — ' Instantly realizing his mistake, he groaned out loud.

'I'm so glad you mentioned that.' She rested both forearms on his chest, then placed her chin on her hands to look him squarely in the eye. It was time to lighten the mood. 'Now tell me,' she began, liberally laying on the skepticism, 'how can I possibly believe a man who professes to love me when he won't trust me with something as intimate as his Q?'

Dan rolled his eyes heavenward. 'Me and my big mouth.'

'Daniel *Quinn* Wilder?' she hazarded another guess.

'Nope.'

'Dan, there are no more Q names.'

'Of course there are.'

'Oh, yeah? Name one.'

He raised his chin as if to say *okay*. 'Quasar.'

She shook her head in exasperation. 'Stop being silly and give me just one hint and I'll leave you alone. For a while.'

He seemed to ponder her request, then agreed with a nod. 'You want a hint? I've got one for you. It means 'one of physical prowess',' he told her with a suggestive arching of one eyebrow.

'Unless you have a book of names with origins and meanings lying around somewhere, that's not fair,' she whined.

'Look,' he said, feigning exasperation. 'Am I giving you a hard time because I don't know your middle name?'

'No, but then I don't have a middle name.'

'You mean it's Kacy No-Middle-Name Angelle.'

'Yes.'

'Tell ya what I'm gonna do,' he offered in a singsong delivery of the standard con-man line. 'You can have joint custody of my Q.'

'I don't know,' she hedged. 'What if it's something perfectly awful?'

'Well, just for you we'll make it something . . . sweet . . . something *you*.' As quickly as he'd gone silly on her, he was serious again. 'Kacy *Querida* Angelle.'

Kacy had read enough historical romances to recognize the Spanish derivative of 'beloved.' Smiling, she said, 'I think I can live with that.' And she thanked him for his gift with a kiss that would have ended in another bout of lovemaking if Dan's stomach hadn't rumbled.

'Just my body's way of reminding me that I haven't lollygagged around in bed after sunrise in . . . well, in more years than I care to admit. Besides, all things stop for a hungry stomach. Remember?' He dragged her out of bed behind him.

They showered together, using all the hot water, dressed, and began breakfast.

'Look,' Dan whispered, standing at the window. Kacy joined him, and to her delight saw that the backyard was filled with squirrels. 'There's Bullwinkle,' he said, pointing to the large fox squirrel closest to the cabin. 'He doesn't look any worse for wear,' he told her, pulling her closer to him and pointing through the window. 'That's Natasha, and Boris, and — '

'Don't tell me,' Kacy interrupted. 'Rocky.'

'Actually, that's Mr. Peabody. Rocky's over there with Dudley and Sweet Nell.' He pointed to another small cluster of the furry creatures. 'If you haven't guessed, I'm a big fan of Rocky and Bullwinkle.'

'No kidding?' she said with a giggle.

'Do you think I'd scare them off if I went out for a closer look?'

'Just don't make any sudden moves. They're pretty used to Ray and me, so you should be able to get fairly close. I'll let you know when breakfast's ready.' They gave each other a hug and Kacy left him to their meal.

Outside, although still chilly, the sun warmed the sky and the damp leaves beneath her feet muffled the sound of her footsteps as she eased up on the family of squirrels blissfully scampering from one pile of feed to the next. Finding a lawn chair, she sat down to watch the antics of the tiny animals who flitted from feed to tree to the woodstack. Two fluffy tails disappeared into a knothole about halfway up a large pine. Kacy filled her lungs with fresh morning air, remembering the day on the river when Dan had told her that if she was very quiet and still she could hear God speaking to her, could feel His sweet breath on her skin. Never had she felt so at peace. Or so keenly alive.

Suddenly, remembering how Ted had insinuated himself into her life during a time when she needed someone, she knew why she had fought her feelings for Dan for so long. She had loved and trusted Ted simply because it had been in her nature to do so, had willingly gone with him only to be emotionally and physically abused to the point of almost losing herself.

And Dan — she smiled to herself with the memories — had forced her into his world, frightened her at first with brutish demands and brooding secrets. Gradually he had stormed her emotions with all the tenderness and love that was in him.

So lost was she in thought that it didn't immediately dawn on her how quiet it had grown. Glancing up, she saw nothing but empty woods where fifteen or twenty squirrels had been playing only moments ago. Disappointed by their desertion, she stood, turned — and bumped into the solid wall of John Broussard. At first, because she recognized the shirt, she thought it was Dan, but then his beefy hands grabbed her arms and panic rose within her.

Jerking free, she put four quick steps between them. His eyes raked the length of her, and Kacy had to fight down the panic again. She said a silent thank-you that Dan was just inside. All she had to do was call for him . . .

'You're comin' with me.' His words struck terror in her heart.

'Dan's just inside,' she threatened, hoping that the mention of Dan would make Broussard think twice about whatever was on his mind. She took another step away.

He grinned and closed the distance with two large paces of his own. 'I ain't worried 'bout Wilder.' He said it so calmly that Kacy's first thought was that he'd done something to Dan.

'Dan!' she screamed, her voice piercing the morning silence of the bottom. Broussard was on her before she could make another move. His fingers bit into the tender flesh of her arms as he dragged her toward the front of the cabin. Inside, she heard Dan calling her name, heard the sickening sound of the iron gate straining against the lock. Kacy and Dan's eyes met and held. He pushed, then pulled against the gate, his face a mirror of the terror she felt when they both realized that he was locked inside.

Broussard grabbed Kacy around the middle, holding her so tightly that it was hard for her to breathe. He laughed and the sound was the most frightening thing she'd ever heard. He grew suddenly quiet and tossed Dan's key ring to the ground in front of the steps.

Hatred blazed in Dan's eyes. 'All right, Broussard, what the hell do you want?' Kacy saw the rage lurking just below his restraint.

Kacy couldn't see Broussard's face but heard the satisfaction in his voice. 'The money.' As if to punctuate his demand, he clamped one hand over Kacy's breast and squeezed. She tried not to wince. It was what he wanted, what he needed to get to Dan. 'The hundred thousand dollars you took from that bank in Houston.'

Dan's face was a reflection of the agony Kacy tried not to show. 'There wasn't any hundred thousand dollars, John.' It was the only time she'd heard Dan call the man by his first name. He was trying to stall, to give her time to find a way to get free. She tried with all that was in her, but Broussard's grip was too strong.

'The whole thing was a personal vendetta between me and the banker,' Dan was saying. 'The hundred thousand was a smokescreen, his way of covering his own ass. All I took was my own money, and I don't even have that any more.'

Again Broussard squeezed, and this time Kacy went limp from pain. 'Don't bullshit me, man,' he growled.

Kacy couldn't see through haze caused by the pain, but she heard Dan's angry voice. 'Don't hurt her.' Then more calmly, 'I don't have that money, John, but I'll get whatever you want.' There was a long pause before he added, 'Just don't hurt her.'

Broussard began dragging Kacy toward the river. 'All right,' he called over Kacy's protests. 'You know where to find me, but I warn you, Wilder, turn on me and you ain't gonna like what you get back.'

'Kacy!' she heard Dan calling. 'Where's the key?'

She tried to answer, but the breath was knocked out of her when Broussard threw her into the bottom of his pirogue. The boat rocked precariously beneath her struggles. A sudden blow to the side of her head forced her to lie still.

'Stay down, bitch, if you don't want more of the same.' With that, Broussard pushed off and Kacy felt the pitching motion of the small craft gliding from shore.

Then she heard the sound of a shotgun blast. Over the edge of the pirogue, she saw Dan burst from the cabin and race for the river. Broussard saw it, too, and Kacy had never seen such fear in a man's face before. If she could get out now, before the water was too deep, even though she couldn't swim, she could make it back to shore. No sooner did she raise up than she saw Broussard draw his paddle high overhead to strike her. Reflexively she cowered in the bottom of the boat, waiting for the blow that never landed.

Instead, she heard Broussard scream, looked up to see the paddle tangled in low-hanging branches overhead, saw the large brownish-black snake fall from its sunning place on top of Broussard. The cottonmouth struck like lightning, hitting him repeatedly in the face and neck, then on his hands when he jerked it free of his head. Broussard fell from the boat, still struggling with the water moccasin. At last the reptile slithered away, leaving a small wake in the water as it made its escape.

Kacy saw that Broussard was in

shock. Blood streamed from the numerous fang marks on his face as he grabbed for the boat.

'Help me!' he screamed, panic making him crazy-wild.

Forgetting everything except that he was a man in trouble, Kacy leaned over the side and reached out for him. Too late, she realized her mistake. Broussard grabbed hold of her, yanked with the strength of a madman. The pirogue was out from under her before she knew it.

There wasn't time to scream. Icy water swirled around her as she toppled out and went under. She managed to free herself of Broussard and resurfaced.

From somewhere she heard Dan calling out to her. 'Try to get to the boat!' She couldn't see the pirogue; she had no idea which way shore lay. Again the muddy waters of the Sabine pulled her under and into the current she knew was taking her farther from shore and from Dan. Everything was muddy-dark, and she felt no pain, no cold. Nothing.

And then there were hands grabbing at her, pulling her along until she lay on soggy ground. 'Come on, Kacy, don't give up on me now.'

She recognized Dan's voice, and the stark fear it held. Roughly she was rolled onto her stomach, and she felt a forceful pressure just below her shoulder blades. As both her elbows were pushed up and forward, she coughed and finally expelled the river water that had threatened to kill her.

'Thank God,' Dan said, turning her over to cradle her in trembling arms.

'Broussard . . . ?' she managed between coughs.

'He made it out of the river, but panicked while I was trying to get to you.' He held her more tightly. 'He ran off into the woods. He'll be dead in a matter of minutes.'

She remembered the cottonmouth and the number of times Broussard had been struck, and couldn't hold back the series of shudders that overtook her. Vile, wretched man that he was, no one deserved to die like that.

The sound of an outboard motor rounding the bend brought Dan's head up. Kacy managed to sit up just in time to see Mr. Fontenot's small boat easing into shore. Another man, one who looked completely out of place in his dark business suit, stepped out into ankle-deep water and approached them.

Kacy felt Dan's body stiffen before he lifted her into his arms.

'Michaelson,' he said, the chill in his greeting more frigid than the water she'd just been dragged from. 'Why aren't I surprised to see you?'

The man he called Michaelson seemed to ignore Dan's sarcasm. 'Is this Miss Angelle under all that mud and moss?'

Kacy wasn't sure how to respond. She knew from Ray's letter who Michaelson was. To tell the truth would put Dan in danger of being arrested for kidnapping.

Dan took the decision from her. 'Yes, but she has nothing to do with all this. I — '

'Let's talk inside,' Michaelson interrupted.

'I'll wait out here, me,' Mr. Fontenot called from behind them.

Inside, Dan wrapped Kacy in a blanket from the bed, pulled the recliner closer to the fire, then got her a mug of steaming coffee. Only then did he offer Michaelson a cup.

Accepting the coffee, Michaelson stood between Kacy and the door until Dan took a seat on the hearth.

'How'd you find me?' Dan wanted to know.

Michaelson sat on the foot of the rumpled bed, his face as serious as his somber charcoal suit. 'I knew the minute Leanne left Colorado that she was coming back to check on you.' He dropped his gaze and studied his shoes with great interest. He was embarrassed about something. 'I lost her in the airport, though, and had to wait until she left for home late last night to talk to her.'

Kacy saw anger flare briefly in Dan's eyes.

'Hawkins is dead,' the lawman said abruptly, drawing the fire to another topic. 'And a contract's been put out on you. When I explained things to Leanne, she saw the danger immediately and told me where to find you.' He cooled his coffee by blowing on it, then took a sip. 'No one else knows that I've talked with Leanne, and that's why I'm here alone.' Glancing around the room, his eyes took in every intimate detail, right down to Kacy's underwear lying beside the bed.

'I'm going to assume, Miss Angelle, that you're here of your own free will.' He waited for her nod. 'Good. What's going on between you and me, Wilder, can be dealt with, but kidnapping — '

'What's on your mind, Michaelson?' Obviously Dan was becoming impatient.

A look that Kacy astutely labeled as remorse swept Michaelson's face. 'I haven't had a good night's sleep since Ray died, Wilder, and I'm doing my damnedest to make things right by Leanne and the boys. And by you.

'We've gotten into Hawkins' files, but until we can get enough information to get the warrants, you'll be in danger. I have to find a way to keep you safe. I don't want any more Wilder blood on my hands.'

Dan exchanged glances with Kacy, and she saw that he was having a hard time dealing with the other man he felt was responsible for Ray's death. But Kacy saw past all that. This man was here to help Dan, whether Dan wanted help or not. A plan began to formulate in her mind.

'Mr. Michaelson,' she said, drawing Dan's and Michaelson's attention.

'It's Detective Michaelson,' he corrected her.

She acknowledged the correction. 'What would happen if the people looking for Dan thought he was dead?'

Both men looked at her like she was seriously brain damaged. 'Think about it, Dan. With the beard, Broussard looks a little like you. Same size and build, same color hair. His billfold is even here, in the bathroom where he left it, so he doesn't have any identification on him. And,' she stretched out the word for effect, 'he's wearing your clothes, the same clothes you were wearing that day.'

The room was deathly quiet. 'Don't you see?' she asked them both. 'We can make it look like *you* were killed by the snake.'

Michaelson's interest was piqued. 'What's she talking about, Wilder?'

Obviously still having his doubts, Dan explained about Broussard. He left out nothing, including the snake attack and the fact that Broussard had been run out of New Orleans after living there for several years.

'Sounds like a good idea ta me.'

All three whipped around to see Mr.

Fontenot standing in the doorway. 'I ain't real sure what's goin' on, me, but if tellin' a little white lie'll keep Dan safe, I'll identify Broussard's body as Dan's.'

Appearing only slightly nonplussed, Michaelson stood. 'This could work.' A grin started and grew with each passing second. 'No one else in the Bureau knows that I've talked with Leanne or that I know where you are. I just *might* be able to pull this off.' He began pacing around the room, talking more to himself than to the other three people there. 'If I can convince enough people that you're dead, the mob will have no reason to keep looking for you.' He turned his back, then spun around again. 'You're sure this man, Broussard, doesn't have any family?'

Fontenot took it upon himself to answer. 'I knowed four generations of Broussards, and John's da last of da line. T'ank da Lord.' He cut his brown eyes at the FBI agent. 'It won't be no great loss, and it'll be a chance for John ta redeem hisself for a passel of wrongs he done, even if he dead and it not his idea.'

'Done.' Michaelson said, sealing Dan's fate as neatly as that. 'Which way did he run?' he asked Dan.

'Behind the cabin.' Dan's eyes were on Kacy's stricken face.

'I'll help you find him,' Fontenot offered, leading the way out. 'But if you'n me goin' ta be partners in crime, I t'ink you better call me Percival.' He gave Michaelson his hand.

'Hugo,' the detective answered, gripping the outstretched hand.

The older man shook his head in disgust. 'Danged if dat ain't bad as mine.'

Alone, Dan and Kacy felt the tiny room closing in on them. Kacy had saved his life, but at what cost. She felt numb with a combination of relief and despair.

'I can't ask you to go into hiding with me . . . ' he began. 'It wouldn't be fair to you or to Mandy. And until I'm sure

Hawkins' bunch is convinced — '

Kacy silenced him by walking into his arms. 'Do you think it'll work?' She felt his chin resting on top on her head, heard his heart beating beneath her ear.

'I think there's a good chance.'

'Then that's all that matters.'

'Wilder.'

They broke apart to find Michaelson waiting outside on the porch. 'We found him not fifty feet away. He's dead all right, and looks pretty bad. Even his own mother wouldn't be able to ID him.' He took one step inside and cleared his throat. 'Are you ready to go, Miss Angelle?'

Dan's hold tightened. 'I'll take her back.'

Michaelson's expressionless gaze didn't waver one iota. 'No,' he said flatly. 'She goes back with us. You need to clear out of here as soon as possible. The place'll be crawling with investigators before nightfall. I hear you have a pretty secluded cabin in Colorado. I'll let Leanne know what's going on so she can help on that end. Leave your billfold here and get rid of Broussard's. And leave everything just like it is.' He looked like he wanted to say more. 'Good luck' was all he said as he stepped back out onto the porch and waited.

'Maybe it's better this way,' Dan said the moment they were alone. 'This isn't good-bye — '

Kacy silenced him with her lips pressed against his. Her chest felt like her heart was being ripped out of it.

'I'll never see a rainbow that I don't remember . . . ' Before she lost her courage to do what was best for Dan, she broke free from him and walked out the door without a backward glance. Michaelson steadied her at the top step. The next thing she knew, she was sitting beside a corpse in Fontenot's boat as it sped upriver.

'I love you, Q,' she whispered, knowing that God's breath would carry it to him.

13

A late-afternoon garden wedding after a May shower was the perfect way to start a new life. The rainbow that arched high overhead in the clearing Texas sky was the crowning glory.

And Kacy remembered.

'Do you, Hugo Frederick Michaelson, take this woman . . . ' The minister's words fuzzed out to a gentle buzzing noise in Kacy's ears. Tears she had promised she wouldn't shed slid down her cheeks and Mandy gave her hand a gentle squeeze. Looking down at the child, Kacy knew she had so much to be thankful for. Today was Mother's Day and she was now legally Mandy's mother, and, after a lengthy investigation and hearing, she and Mary were finally the rightful owners of their business. Wee Care was thriving, as were many other smaller day-care centers now that the Bright and Early centers were closed. It seemed that Marcus Hawkins had dipped heavily into the mob's reserve to finance his wife's enterprises.

'And, do you, Mary Catherine Ann Martin, take this man . . . '

Giving herself a mental shake, Kacy brought her attention back to her friend's wedding. Mary was a dream to behold in her shimmery white moiré evening dress and mini-veil. Mike, as Mary insisted on calling Michaelson, saying that Hugo didn't suit him and that she'd be damned if she'd spend the rest of her life with someone called Fred, was anything but his usual calm and collected self in his white tuxedo. In spite of the mild seventy-degree weather, a fine beading of perspiration sprinkled his forehead and a grim expression masked his handsome features.

Kacy smiled, remembering all the hours she and Mary had spent with the very professional, overly poised

Detective Michaelson those first few weeks. When there didn't seem to be any reason for them to go to his office to give statements any longer, he started dropping by Wee Care several times a week, taking Mary to lunch. From there it progressed to dinner out once, then twice a week, and then he seemed to become a permanent fixture in the evenings at Mary's small house.

Perfect for each other was how she would describe the handsome couple exchanging wedding vows beside her. Just like she'd thought that she and Dan were —

Not today, she commanded herself. She wouldn't ruin the day for Mary by feeling sorry for herself.

'You may kiss your bride.'

A loud hoopla rose from the crowd and the music began again. Laughing, talking friends and relatives crowded in, and Kacy gave the happy couple quick hugs and kisses and made her way through the throng of well-wishers.

Standing to one side now with

Mandy impatiently tugging at her hand, Kacy watched her friends. Mike was smiling now, truly smiling and laughing. He grabbed Mary around her tiny waist and gave her a twirl of celebration. Everyone hooted their approval. Tears of joy streamed unchecked down Kacy's face as she laughed with the others.

'Mommy,' Mandy called above the din of merry-making. 'May I go play with Haylee and Brittany?'

'Of course, honey.' Kacy was glad they'd invited their Wee Care children and families. It wouldn't have been the same without them there to share the joy. 'Just stay here in the backyard. I'll fix you a plate and find you soon.' Mandy gave her a kiss and skipped away.

'Kacy,' Mary called, threading her way through the crowd, 'it's time for the pictures. Where's Mandy?' Whiskey-colored eyes scanned the milling crowd. 'Never mind. We'll get her later. Are you all right?'

Kacy cursed herself for letting her self-pity show. 'Why wouldn't I be all right?' she countered with a smile that was only slightly forced. 'My best friend just married the best man in Harris County.'

They knew each other too well, and Mary's face softened with understanding. 'He'll be back,' she said, taking Kacy's hand in her own.

'No, Mary.' Kacy tried to act as though she'd accepted it. 'If he hasn't come back by now . . . ' She couldn't make herself say out loud what she'd thought for months.

Their parting had been so abrupt that the whole experience seemed like a dream now, almost as if it had never happened. For months she had lain in bed at night, remembering how shaken Dan had looked when she stepped away and walked out the door with Mike.

From that point on, Mike had called all the shots, had personally covered every aspect of the investigation. The only rough spots had come during

Kacy's questioning: Had she known the man who had abducted her? No, she'd answered without hesitation, she had seen him only the one other time in the bank. How had he gotten them to the secluded cabin? Thinking it safer to stick as close to the truth as possible, she told them about switching cars at the refinery, the drive through the storm and the river bottom, and about the dreaded canoe trip. The investigating team hadn't found the pickup until a few weeks later, abandoned in Lake Charles. Could she account for that? The only thing she could think of, she told them, was that someone had stolen it. She then related the story of the hunter who had been stranded, and how, after her abductor gave him shelter, the keys to his truck had disappeared. No, she didn't remember the hunter's name, and she hadn't enlisted his help because she'd been more frightened of him than of Dan.

And the door, they wanted to know, why had its lock been blasted away?

Dan had locked her inside while he planned an excursion out of the bottom. He'd forgotten about the shotgun he'd left out after cleaning it. When she saw the snake attack Dan, then watched him run off in a panic, she knew that she was stranded. No one knew she was there; she had to get out.

Then they got personal. In all that time, had Dan hurt her? No, she answered emphatically. He had frightened her, but he had never harmed her in any way.

Seeming satisfied with her answers, they apologized for putting her through the ordeal of questioning and let her go home.

Mike had been pleased with her answers, but as the months passed and he couldn't talk with her about the case any longer, she stopped asking about Dan, too. And when she didn't hear from Dan, she'd come to the only conclusion that made even the slightest sense to her: He and Leanne were probably raising Ray's children together. Somehow it was easier thinking of him as settled and living a family life in the Rocky Mountains than to envision him still on the run, never having a moment's peace.

Someone called Mary's name and she turned and answered, 'We'll be right there.' Then to Kacy, 'I have a surprise for you later. If it ever gets here,' she muttered under her breath. 'But first things first.' She stood back to appraise Kacy with deep affection and a critical eye. 'When we picked out this suit, I never dreamed you'd hide that darling camisole by buttoning the jacket all the way up to your nose.' The white linen suit hugged every graceful curve that Kacy seemed determined to hide.

'That *darling camisole* is cut so low that I'd die of embarrassment,' Kacy retorted, recalling just how provocative the white satin spaghetti-strap under-blouse truly was. She was thankful for the full-sleeved cardigan jacket and its two dozen tiny covered buttons that went from the hem of the jacket to the modest neckline.

'I wish you'd loosen up once in a while,' Mary chided, dragging Kacy along behind her to where the photographer waited with the rest of the wedding party. Having eloped for her first marriage, Mary had wanted to wear white today — and had insisted that all her attendants do the same. Even the weather was kind enough to cooperate. The group was a splash of white against a clear blue sky, the only other color that of the Saint Augustine grass and the greenery in the bouquets carried by the bride and her bridesmaids. Even the ribbons and bows in the flowers placed strategically about the yard were pearly white.

Time dragged by for Kacy, and once or twice she saw Mary and Mike glance at their watches, their expressions serious as they bent their heads together. No doubt they were plotting their escape from the reception that gave no evidence of winding down.

An hour later, all the pictures were taken, Mary had seen to it that Kacy caught the bridal bouquet and an enthusiastic bachelor she couldn't see snagged the groom's garter out of midair. Mandy and all the children had been fed, and Kacy milled around the table of food unable to decide what, if anything, she wanted to put on her plate.

'Know where a man could get a bowl of chili and crackers around here?' The voice came from directly behind her.

Every emotion imaginable swarmed Kacy's senses. Six months, an elaborately decorated garden complete with flowers and candles, a five-piece band and dozens of finely dressed guests disappeared when she whirled around to look into the brilliant green eyes that had haunted her every waking and sleeping moment.

Except for the handsomely tailored tuxedo that perfectly fit his tall, powerful body, Daniel Quinlan Wilder was the same. The delicate white garter in his hand stood out in stark relief against his tanned skin.

She didn't know how to react. She wanted to throw herself into his arms and tell him how much she'd missed him, how much she loved him, and how glad she was that he was alive and well. She also wanted to strike out at him for not getting in touch with her sooner. So she did nothing.

'Chili?' she heard Mary saying from behind her.

'Must be a private joke,' Mike answered Mary's question when no one else did. 'Good to see you, Dan.' He extended his hand and the two men greeted each other.

'Is this *him*?' Mary insinuated herself between Kacy and Dan to eye him approvingly before a frown creased her brow. 'You're late.' She didn't try to cover her annoyance. 'I was afraid she was going to leave before you got here. I'm Mary,' she added abruptly with the smile that had dazzled many an unsuspecting male.

Dan took his dressing down like the man he was, then leaned down and kissed the bride. 'I wish you every happiness,' he said, turning to Mike. 'And you,' he began, a twinkle in his eyes, 'lucked out. I wasn't sure if I could believe a man who lies as convincingly as you. She's everything you said she was. Congratulations.'

Kacy was in a daze. Everyone had known that Dan would be here today except her. The band struck up again and Mike took Mary's arm.

'If you two'll excuse us, I believe I promised the first waltz to my wife.'

'Oh, Mikie, we can dance anytime. I want to make sure everything's all right here.'

'Mikie?' Dan looked as confused as Kacy felt.

Mike gave Dan a sheepish look. 'It's a long story.' To Mary, he said, 'Give us all a break, honey. They can fill us in when we get back from the cruise.'

'Hugo,' Dan said, stopping them

before they could leave and handing him a slip of paper. 'Take care of this for me.'

Alone at last with the one man she'd dreamed of seeing again for months, Kacy found herself at a total loss for words. Where did one begin when there were so many questions?

Thankfully Dan labored under no such handicap. 'I'll have to say that you clean up nice,' he said with a nervous laugh, one that Kacy returned. The last time he'd seen her she'd been soaking wet and covered with mud and moss. And, other than that first day in the bank, he'd never seen her in anything other than the long johns or her rumpled clothes — or her skimpy black undies. 'You're more beautiful than I remembered.' That he was sincere there was no doubt, but Kacy barely heard him through the roaring that had started in her ears.

Dan was as observant as ever. 'Are you okay?' He took her arm, led her to an out-of-the-way table, where he helped her into a chair.

Kacy's senses were acutely fine-tuned. A bumblebee buzzed harmlessly around the azaleas at her back; a warm gulf breeze wafted about them, carrying with it the scent of honeysuckle and gardenia. And Dan smelled as wonderful as ever.

'I didn't mean to upset you,' he said from in front of her.

'No,' she finally managed to say. 'You just have a way of knocking my feet out from under me.' She was starting to feel better. Patting the chair beside her, she entreated him, 'Come, sit down. Or do you want me staring at your zipper all afternoon?'

Dan laughed and Kacy knew that all was well. 'Now there's the Kacy I know and love.' Silence fell like a shadow between them again until Dan took her hand in his.

'Have you been well?'

If you don't count a broken heart an illness, she wanted to say. 'Yes,' she managed to get out. 'And you?'

'Don't I look well?' He was teasing her now.

Kacy couldn't suppress a smile. 'You know you do.' Gone was the haggard, haunted look she remembered. He looked rested and healthy and at peace. She tried to take her hand from him. He refused to relinquish it. 'I . . . don't know what to say to you,' she admitted, feeling relieved when he squeezed her fingers gently.

'I know.' He reached over and turned her face toward him. 'Hugo . . . Mike . . . ' He shook his head at the nickname. 'Hugo wouldn't give me the okay to come back to Texas until yesterday. I was on the first plane out this morning.' He wiped away a tear that tracked down her cheek. 'I've never stopped loving you, baby. And not being able to be with you, talk with you, has been the hardest thing I've ever had to do. Even though we were certain the story about my death had been accepted, we couldn't take any chances. If anyone even suspected the truth before every name on that list was behind bars, we'd all have been in danger. You, me, Leanne and the boys.'

There was both truth and wisdom in what he told her, and she wanted to cry for joy. But the mention of Leanne made her cautious.

'And what about Leanne?'

'She's fine. Her baby's due next month.'

'And you left her?'

'Why wouldn't I leave her? She's healthy, the baby's healthy. Besides, you and Mandy and I can go visit when the baby comes.'

'But I thought you and Leanne were . . . that you and she . . . '

Dan stared at her, his expression blank. 'Leanne and me? What are you talking about?'

Kacy began to fidget with the hem of her skirt. She'd gone this far, she might as well lay it all out. 'In Ray's letter he asked you to take care of her and his sons. He even said how happy you and

Leanne could be together.'

The smile she'd longed to see again for so many months crept across his face; then he drew her into his arms. 'Oh, baby. Leanne and I are family. She's like my sister. We could never be more than that, no matter what Ray wanted.'

The band had stopped playing and Mike's voice boomed over the speakers. 'We have a special request, folks, so everybody gather round for this one. I wish I could take credit, Mary, but it goes for me, too.'

The male vocalist hired for the wedding began singing the song Kacy would forever think of as 'their song.' She knew a moment of sheer happiness as Dan stood and held out his hand to her.

'I knew you'd remember.' He took her into his arms and they were the only couple on the dance floor. 'Just like I knew that night we danced in the cabin that I'd fallen in love with you.' His words softly whispered came close to the lyrics of the song, thrilling Kacy no end.

She relived every magic moment of that first dance — and of that night. And, while the memory was vivid and exciting, the touch of Dan's hand on hers, the feel of his arm around her, the fragrance he wore were her world now. His lips at her temple sent a pulsating current sparking between them. She tilted her head back, and, searching his face, knew that their time had come. This dance was only the beginning of the rest of their lives.

'Dan . . . ' It seemed all she could say. Raising her hand to caress his cheek, she met his lips with hers and lost herself over to the wonder that was Dan. Only vaguely aware of the tear-filled eyes watching them, Kacy glanced up, seeing only the man she loved.

'There was a rainbow earlier,' she whispered as the melody played on.

'And now our love song. Everything would be perfect if we had a sorry excuse for a bed.' He held her at distance, then grinned broadly as Mary and Mike joined them on the dance-floor. 'That's a knock-my-socks-off dress, baby, but . . . '

'What?' she wanted to know.

'All those little, bitty buttons are going to be a pain in the . . . button-hole.'

THE END